The Substance o

F. W. Bain

Alpha Editions

This edition published in 2024

ISBN : 9789364731775

Design and Setting By
Alpha Editions
www.alphaedis.com
Email - info@alphaedis.com

INTRODUCTION

I could almost persuade myself, that others will like this little fable as much as I do: so curiously simple, and yet so strangely profound is its delicate epitome of the old old story, the course of true love, which never did run smooth.

And since so many people have asked me questions as to the origin of these stories, I will say a word on the point here. Where do they come from? I do not know. I discovered only the other day that some believe them to have been written by a woman. That appears to me to be improbable. But who writes them? I cannot tell. They come to me, one by one, suddenly, like a flash of lightning, all together: I see them in the air before me, like a little Bayeux tapestry, complete, from end to end, and write them down, hardly lifting the pen from the paper, straight off "from the MS." I never know, the day before, when one is coming: it arrives, as if shot out of a pistol. Who can tell? They may be all but so many reminiscences of a former birth.

The *Substance of a Dream* is half a love-story, and half a fairy tale: as indeed every love-story is a fairy tale. Because, although that unaccountable mystery, the mutual attraction of the sexes, is the very essence of life, and everything else merely accidental or accessory, yet only too often in the jostle of the world, in the trough and tossing of the waves of time, the accidental smothers the essential, and life turns into a commonplace instead of a romance. And so, like every other story, this little story will perhaps be very differently judged, according to the reader's sex. The bearded critic will see it with eyes very different from those with which it may be viewed by the fair voter with no beard upon her chin; for women, as the great god says at the end, have scant mercy on their own sex, and the heroine of the story is a strange heroine, an enigmatical Mona Lisa, so to say, who will not appeal to everybody so strongly as she does to the Moony-crested Deity, when he sums her up at the close. I venture, with humility, to concur in the opinion of the Deity, for she holds me under the same spell as her innumerable other lovers. The reader, a more formidable authority even than the god, must decide: only I must warn him that to understand, he must go to the very end. He will not think his time wasted, if he take half the delight in reading, as I did, in transcribing, the evidence in the case. Only, moreover, when he closes the book will he appreciate the mingled exactitude and beauty of its name: for no story ever had a name which fitted it with such curious precision as this one. For the essence of a dream is always that along with its weird beauty, it counters expectation, often in such queer, ludicrous, kaleidoscopic ways. So it is, here.

Many bitter things, since the beginning, have men said of women, though neither so many nor so bitter, as the witty Frenchman cynically remarks, as the things women have said of one another. Poor Eve has paid very dear for that apple: the only wonder is, that she was not made responsible also for the Flood: but we have not got the whole of that story: Noah's wife may have dropped some incriminating documents into the water, for the Higher Criticism to unearth by and by: the Eternal Feminine may have had a hand in it after all, as she is generally to be found somewhere behind the scenes, wherever mischief brews for mortal man. She comes down the ages, loaded with accusations; and yet, somehow or other, they do not seem to have done her much harm. And the reason is, that she possesses, in supreme perfection, the art of disarming her antagonist, having been very cunningly constructed by the Creator for that very purpose: she is like a cork; she will not drown, under any flood of charges: she floats, *quand même*: (two words that she might very well take, like the inimitable Sarah, for her motto:) so that, be as angry as you please with her, you generally find yourself not only unable to condemn her, but even ready to beg her pardon, and rather glad, on the whole, to get it. It is a hopeless case. And all the more, because no woman ever lived, bad or good, who could be got to understand what is meant by "playing cricket": you cannot make her keep the rules in any game: she plays to win, like a German, and invariably cheats, if she can: international law counts, only as long as it is for and not against her: if you find her out, and scold her, she pouts, and will not play. And then, if, as is commonly the situation, you want her to play, very badly, what are you to do? Yes, it is a hopeless case.

And yet, if we look into the matter with that stern impartiality which its public importance demands, we may perceive, that though there is, it must be candidly owned, an element of truth in the charges brought against her, they are founded, for all that, largely on misunderstanding. It is man himself, her accuser, who is very nearly always to blame. His intelligence as compared with her own, is clumsy: (it is the difference between the dog and the cat:) he does not realise the unfathomable gulf that divides her nature from his own, and for lack of imaginative tact, judging her by himself, he enormously overestimates the part played by reason in her behaviour. Hence when, as she is always doing, she lets him down, he breaks out, (obtusely) into denunciation and reproach, taking it for granted, that what she did, she did, deliberately. But that is his mistake. Women never act by deliberation, least of all in their relations with men. Reason has hardly anything to do with it. A woman is a weapon, designed by the Creator, who generally knows what he is doing, to fascinate the other sex: that is her essence and her *raison d'être*: the woman who does not do it is a failure, and she is Nature's triumph and entelechy, who does it best. And this every woman knows, by instinct, and feels, long before she knows it, almost as soon as she can stand upon her feet: consequently, no artificially elaborated compliment, no calculated flattery, ever touches her so near, as it does, when she perceives that her personality *tells*, acts like a charm, on any given man: a point about which no woman ever blunders, as a man often so ridiculously does about himself: she invariably detects, by unerring instinct, when her arrow hits its mark. And this involuntary homage she finds so irresistibly delectable, going as it does down to the very depths of her being, and endorsing it, that she literally *cannot* deny herself the pleasure of basking in it, making hay, so to say, while her sun shines, revelling in the consciousness of her power all the more delicious because she knows only too well that she must lose it later on, as youth flies: old age, *i.e.* the loss of her charm, being every woman's ogre, the skeleton in her cupboard, which she dreads far more than death, just as the only disease which she shudders to face is the smallpox, for a similar reason. And so, when she finds her spell working, she lets herself go: never dreaming what interpretation her victim puts on her behaviour: and then, all at once, she awakes to discover with what fire she was ignorantly playing. And then it is, that she recoils, on the verge: and then it is, that thwarted in the very moment that he deemed triumph secured, the baffled lover falls into fury and abuse, because he imagines her to have been all along clearly aware of what she was about, which is exactly what hardly one woman in a million does. Not being a man, she does not understand: her end is only his beginning: his object is possession, still to come: hers is already gained in the form of the tribute to her charm: she was only playing (every woman is a child), he was in deadly earnest, and took her purely instinctive self-congratulation for a promise deliberately made. Suddenly illuminated, she lets him down abruptly with a bump, all the harder that she never meant to do it (the *coquette* does: but she is a horrible professional, methodising feminine instinct, for prey: a psychological ghoul, feeding on souls instead of bodies, and deserving extermination without benefit of clergy). The real crime of woman is not so much a crime as a defect: she is weak, as all the sages know, and all languages prove, though "democracy" ignores it; it is her strength, and half her charm, that she cannot stand alone, like a creeper. But that is why you cannot depend on her, good or bad. Irresolution is her essence: she will "determine" one way, and act in another, according to the pressure. Instinct, inclination or aversion, vanity, emotion, pity or fear, or even mere chance: these are her motives, the forces that move her: reason counts with her for absolutely nothing, a thing like arithmetic, useful, even indispensable, but only for adding up a grocer's bill, or catching a train. It has literally nothing to do with her heart. There is no folly like the folly of supposing that it has: yet on this folly rest most of the accusations against her. Reduce her to a rational being, and you degrade her to the level of an inferior man. But she is not his inferior: she is his dream, his magnet, his force, his inspiration, and his fate. Take her away, and you annihilate him: Othello's occupation's gone. Nine-tenths of the great things done in the world have been done for a woman. Why? Exactly because she would burn down a street to boil her baby's milk. No rational being would do that: but we all owe our lives to it.

And hence, misogyny is only a pique. To fall foul of the sea, like Xerxes, when it wrecks your ambitions, is to behave as he did, like a spoiled child, without the child's excuse. "If you burn your fingers, is the flame to blame?" You should have known better. When Aristotle was reproved, by some early political economist, for giving alms to a beggar, he replied: I gave not to the man, but humanity. Admirable retort! which is exactly in point here. When she requited your homage with such encouraging smiles, it was not *you* but the man in you, that appealed to her. And because you are *a* man, are you necessarily *the* man? Not at all. And argument is mere waste of time: reason is not the court of appeal. *If of herself she will not love, nothing can make her.* Yet why draw the poet's ungallant conclusion? Why should *the devil take her*? Because she was weak (were *you* not weak?) is she therefore to be damned beyond redemption? Because flattery was sweet, must she give herself away to every male animal that confesses the spell? Surely that is not only harsh, but preposterous, even outrageous. Are you sure that your merit is worthy of such generosity?

And yet, here is the human catastrophe. Why did the Creator scatter his sexual attraction so anomalously that it is so rarely reciprocated, each lover pursuing so often another who flies him for a third, as in *Midsummer Night's Dream*, an imbroglio oddly enough found in a little poem identical in the Greek Moschus and the Hindoo Bhartrihari? Was it blunder or design? Why could he not have made action and reaction equal and opposite, as they are in mechanics? For if affection could not operate at all, unless it was mutual, there would be no unhappy, because ill-assorted, marriages. What a difference it would have made! Had mutual gravitation been the law of the sexes, as it is of the spheres, this Earth would never have stood in need of a Heaven, since it would have existed already: for the only earthly heaven is a happy marriage. As it is, even when it is not a Hell, a marriage is only too often but an everlasting sigh.

And not marriage only, but life. For here lies the solution of a mystery that has baffled the sages, who have failed to discover it chiefly because they have blinded themselves by their own theological and philosophical delusions, idealism and monotheism. Why is it, that gazing at Nature's inexhaustible beauty, thrown at us with such lavish profusion in her dawns and her sunsets, her shadows and her moods, in the roar of her breakers and the silence of her snows, the gloom of her thunder and the spirit of her hills, the blue of her distance and the tints of her autumns, the glory of her blossom and the dignity of her decay, her heights and her abysses, her fury and her peace—why is it, that as we gaze insatiably at these never ending miracles, we are haunted by so unaccountable a sadness, which is not in the things themselves, for Nature never mourns, but in some element that we ourselves import? For if the Soul be only Nature's mirror, her looking-glass, whence the melancholy? It is because beneath our surface consciousness, far away down below, in the dark organic depths that underlie it, we feel without clearly understanding that, as the Hindoos put it, we have missed the fruit of our existence, owing to our never having found our other half. For every one of us, so far from being a self-sufficient whole, an independent unity, is incomplete, requiring for its metaphysical satisfaction, its complement, apart from which it never can attain that peace which passeth all understanding, for which it longs obscurely, and must ever be uneasy, till it finds it. For just as no misfortunes whatever can avail to mar the bliss of the man who has beside him the absolute sympathy of his feminine ideal, so on the other hand no worldly success of any kind can compensate for its absence. All particular causes of happiness or misery are swallowed up and sink into insignificance and nullity compared with this: this present, they disappear: this absent, each alone is sufficient to wreck the soul, fluttering about without rudder or ballast on the waves of the world. Duality is the root, out of which alone, for mortals, happiness can spring. And the old Hindoo mythology, which is far deeper in its simplicity than the later idealistic pessimism, expresses this beautifully by giving to every god his other half; the supreme instance of which dualism is the divine Pair, the Moony-crested god and his inseparable other half, the Daughter of the Snow: so organically symbolised that they coalesce indistinguishably into one: the *Arddanárí*, the Being half Male half Female, He whose left half is his wife. That is the true ideal: cut in two, and destroyed, by the dismal inhuman monotheism of later sophistical speculation.

It was long before I understood this: the solution came to me suddenly, of its own accord, as all profound solutions always come, apparently by accident: like a "fluke" in a game of skill, where often unskilfulness unintentionally does something that could not be achieved by any degree of skill whatever, short of the divine.[1] And the two things that combined to produce my spark of illumination were, as it so fell out, the two things that mean most to me, a sunset and a child. The child was looking at the sunset, and I was looking at the child. Some readers of these stories have been introduced to her before, and will be obliged to me for renewing the acquaintance, as they would be to the postman who brought them news of an old friend.

The sunset was like every other sunset, the garment of a dying deity, and a gift of god: but it had a special peculiarity of its own, and it was this strange peculiarity that arrested the attention of the child. For children are little animals, *terram spectantia*, taking sunsets and other commonplaces such as mother, father, home, furniture and carpets, generally for granted, being as a rule absorbed in the great things of life, that is, play. This child was very diligently blowing bubbles, occasionally turning aside up a by-path to make a bubble-pudding in the soap-dish: the ruckling noise of this operation possessing some magical fascination for all childhood. And in the meanwhile, yellow dusk was gradually deepening in the quiet air. Presently the tired sun sank like a weight, red-hot, burning his way down through filmy layers of Indian ink. The day had been rainy, but the clouds had all dissolved imperceptibly away into a broken chain of veils of mist, which looked with the sun behind them like dropping showers of liquid gold, or copper-coloured waterfalls: while underneath or through them the lines of low blue hills showed now half obscured, now clear and sharp in outline as if cut with scissors out of paper and stuck upon the amber background of the sky. And then came the miracle. Right across the horizon, a little higher than the sun, a long thin bar of cloud suddenly changed colour, becoming rich dark purple, and all along its jagged upper edge the light shot out in one continuous sheet of bright glory to the zenith, while below there poured from the bar a long cascade, a very Niagara of golden mist and rain, as if the flood-gates of some celestial dam had suddenly given way, and all the precious stuff were escaping in a cataract through the rift, in one gigantic plunge, to be lost for ever in some bottomless abyss.

Suddenly, the dead silence struck me: my ear missed the "ruckle," and the occasional exclamations of delight. I turned abruptly, and glanced at the child. She was standing still as a stone, with one hand just in front of her holding the forgotten pipe, arrested on the way to her mouth, as the heavenly vision struck her: rapt, lost in her eyes, which were filled with wonder to the brim, open-mouthed, entranced, with a smile on her lips of which she was totally unconscious, faint, involuntary, seraphic, indescribable. The ecstasy of union had swallowed her: she was gone. I called her by her name: she never heard: her soul was away at the golden gates.

And I said to myself, as I gazed at her with intense curiosity, mixed with regret that I was not Raffael, so marvellous was the picture: This, this is the wisdom of the sages, the secret of Plotinus and the Buddhists: this is

Nirwána, Moksha, Yoga, the unattainable ecstasy of bliss, the absolute fruition, which men call by many names: the end towards which the adult strives, in vain, to recover what he lost by ceasing to be a child: a child, which is sexless, knowing as yet nothing of the esoteric dissatisfaction of the soul that wants and has not found. Aye! to reach the mystic union, the absolute extinction of the Knower in the All; to lose one's Self in Infinity, without a remnant of regret; to attain to the unattainable, the point of self-annihilation where all distinction between subject and object, something and nothing, disappears, it is necessary to be a child: to be born again. *Rebirth*! the key to the enigma of unhappiness lies there!

And after a while, as I watched her, she came back to herself. Our eyes met: and she looked at me long, with a far-off expression that I could not define. And at last, she gave a little sigh. Daddy, she said, why does the golden rain never fall here? Our rain is always only common rain.

And I said solemnly: Little girls are the reason why. But she didn't understand. She looked at me reproachfully with puzzled eyes—such great, grey, beautiful, sea-green eyes!—and then drew a long breath. And she went back to her bubbles, and together we watched them go as they floated away into the valley, wild with excitement as to whether my bubble or her bubble would go farthest before it burst—till the Rhadamanthine summons came, and the Bubble-Blower went to bed.

Poona, 1919.

FOOTNOTES:

[1] *O quantum est subitis casibus ingenium!* an exquisite line of Martial which ought to be posted on a board on every putting-green.

I
ON THE BANKS OF GANGES

BENEDICTION

What! the Digit of the Moon on his brow, Gangá in his hair, and Gaurí on his knee, and yet proof against all Love's arrows! O wonder of wonders! who but the greatest of all the gods would not have melted long ago, like butter between three fires?[2]

Now, long ago, it happened, that Párwatí was left alone on Kailàs for a little while, as she waited for the Lord of the Moony Tire. And having nothing else to do, she amused herself by building an elephant of snow, with large ears and a little tail, made of a yak's hair. And when it was finished, she was so delighted with her toy, that she began to clap her hands: and then, not being able to endure waiting, she went off with impatience to fetch the Moony-crested god, to show him what she had done, and revel in his applause. And the moment that her back was turned, Nandi[3] happened to come along: and just as he reached the elephant, which owing to his abstraction he never noticed, taking it for a mere hump, formed at random by the snowdrifts, he was suddenly seized with an irresistible desire to roll. And so, over he rolled, and went from side to side, throwing up his legs into the air. And as luck would have it, exactly at that very moment the Daughter of the Snow returned, pulling Maheshwara along eagerly by the hand. And she looked and saw Nandi, rolling about on the flat snow just where she had left her elephant, which was gone. And she uttered a loud cry, and stood, aghast with rage and disappointment. And she opened her mouth to curse the author of the mischief, and was on the very verge of saying: Sink into a lower birth, thou insolent destroyer! when Maheshwara stopped her in the very act, guessing her intention, by putting his hand upon her mouth.[4] And he exclaimed: Say nothing rash, O angry one, for Nandi did not do it on purpose, after all. And a good servant does not deserve cursing, for an accidental blunder.

And then, Párwatí burst into tears. And she exclaimed: Out of my sight, thou clumsy one! for I cannot bear to see thee. And she turned away, sobbing. And Maheshwara looked at her out of the corner of his eye, and he said to himself: Now, then, I must do something to console her for the elephant, and bring back her good humour. For ill humour in a woman spoils all. And presently he said: Come now, enough! for Nandi has gone off in disgrace, sufficiently punished by banishment for a time, and very sad to have been the unwitting cause of thy distress. And let us roam about awhile, in search of something new, that may help to obliterate recollection, and change thy gloom into a smile.

And he took the goddess in his arms, and set her as she sobbed upon his knee, and rose from the peak of Kailàs, and shot like a falling star down into the plain below. And coming to Haradwára, where Gangá issues from the hills, he began to follow the holy stream down its course, gliding along just above it like a cloud that was unable to refrain from watching its own beautiful reflection in the blue mirror of her wave. And so they went, until at last they reached an island that was nothing but a sandbank in the very middle of the river, covered with crocodiles lying basking in the sun. And then he said: See! we will go down, and rest awhile among the crocodiles on this sand, whose banks resemble nothing so much as the outline of thy own graceful limbs. And Umá said tearfully: Pish! what do I care for crocodiles, that sit for hours never even moving, like a *yogí* in a trance?

Then said the cunning god: None the less, we will go down: for it may be that the island contains something besides its crocodiles. And as they settled on it, he said again: Did I not say we should find something? for yonder it lies, and it is a very great curiosity indeed. And now, canst thou tell me what it is?

And she looked at it with scrutiny, and presently she said: I can tell this only, that it must have been in the water for a very long time, before it was washed up at last upon this bank by the river's flood: since it is but a shapeless lump, covered with sand and rust and dirt. Who but thyself could even guess what it might be? And Maheshwara said: It has had a very long journey, and been not only in the river, but in a crocodile too. For crocodiles swallow everything. And long ago, this was carried by a man, who was drowned in another stream by the upsetting of his boat, and became with all he carried the prey of an old crocodile, which died long ago, and rotted away, letting this at last escape out of its tomb, and roll along, till at last it got into the Ganges, and was thrown up here in the rainy season, only the other day. And when at last the water sank, lo! there it lay, as it has lain until this moment, as if expecting thy arrival, to provide thee with entertainment. And when all is over, thou wilt very likely bless Nandi, instead of cursing him; since but for his awkwardness in rolling on thy elephant, thou wouldst never have known anything about it.

And Párwatí said peevishly: Where is the entertainment in this foolish lump of flotsam, of which thou hast related the adventures without ever saying what it is?

And the Moony-crested god said: Aha! Snowy One, do not be too sure. For many things hold in their heart things not to be anticipated, judging by their outside: and this lump which thou despisest is like a coco-nut, whose coarse skin is full of nectar. But it has been shut so long, that it would not easily be opened by anyone but me.[5] And he touched it with his foot, saying, Open, and it opened like a shell. And he said: See! it has in it a very strange kernel, preserved safe and sound only because all its adventures added to its case, sheath after sheath. And all the leaves are still there, a very little mouldy, and the silk that tied them, and the seal. And the goddess said: But what is it after all? And Maheshwara said: It is a case of urgency, that all came to nothing in the end, being a letter that never even reached its destination, because the sender was in so great a hurry that he defeated his own object, bidding his messenger go so fast that in his haste his boat turned over, and he and his message were eaten on their way by a river beast. For those who go too fast often go so slow as never to arrive at all, as was the case here. Then said Umá: He that sent it must have been a fool. And Maheshwara said! Nay, O Snowy One, not at all: far from it: and yet he became, as many do, a fool for the occasion, under the influence of passion, which blinds the eyes, and shuts up the ears, and twists the whole character awry, so that it acts in a manner contrary to itself, as if the man had been suddenly changed into another, or his body entered by a Wetála, in the temporary absence of his soul.

And Párwatí said: What was the passion here? And the Moony-crested god said slowly: It was a threefold cord, and very strong: love, and love turned by intense disappointment into hatred, and rage against a rival: each by itself alone enough to turn reason into madness. But the whole story is told, by its hero himself, in the very letter: and if thou wilt, I will read it aloud to thee, exactly as he wrote it, word for word. And the goddess said: Thou knowest all: why not tell it in thy own way, without the trouble of reading? And Maheshwara said: Nay, on the contrary, it is far better to let him tell it for himself: for who knew everything better than he did? And moreover, every story told by a stranger is imperfect, since he is obliged to fill up the gaps in his knowledge by imagination or conjecture: whereas, when the actor in it all is himself the narrator, it is the very truth itself, unless he expressly desires to conceal it, which is not the case here. For he was very anxious indeed to tell his enemy everything, on purpose to offend him: and he only made one mistake, which I will show thee in due time. So I will read it exactly as it stands, omitting absolutely nothing. And the Daughter of the Snow said: Read. But she thought: If it is not worth hearing, I will simply go to sleep as he reads. And Maheshwara said: Nay, O Snowy One, I will guarantee that thou dost not go to sleep.

And then, the goddess suddenly threw her arms about his neck, and hid her face on his breast. And she said: What is the use of trying to hide anything at all from thee? Read. But for all that, I will go to sleep, if I choose. And the Moony-crested god said with a smile: Aye! but thou wilt not choose.

And then he began to read, throwing away the leaves as they ended, one by one into the stream, which carried them away. And the crocodiles all lay round him in a circle, worshipping their Lord, as he read.

FOOTNOTES:

[2] Maheshwara is the ascetic *par excellence*, who punished Love for trying to tempt him by burning him up like a moth with a fiery glance from his third eye. And yet for all that, the Master Yogi was not always proof against feminine fascination: he might be chaste as ice, yet he has not escaped scandal.

[3] Nandi is the divine Bull, on which, or whom, the Great God rides.

[4] Had the awful words passed her lips, Nandi was a doomed bull, as a curse once uttered is irrevocable.

[5] Because he is the Lord of Creatures animate or inanimate, which all obey him.

II
THE HEART OF A WOMAN

I

As the black cobra sits up, and puffs his hood, and hisses, giving warning to his prey, ere he strikes: so I, Shatrunjaya[6] the lute-player, son of a king, do send this my menace to thee, Narasinha, the lover of a queen too good for so vile a thing as thou art: that none hereafter may be able to say, I struck thee unwarned, or took thee unawares. Know, that night doth not more surely or more swiftly follow day, than I and my vengeance will follow on the messenger who carries this threat: whom I have bidden to reach thee with his utmost speed, so as to allay my thirst for thy life; since every day that I wait seems to me longer than a *yuga*. And I will slay thee with no other weapon than my two bare hands—

And suddenly, the great god stopped, and he laughed aloud. And he exclaimed: See now, how this poor lute-player deceived himself! For his message not only never reached his enemy at all, but almost as soon as it had left him, he was himself slain by the emissaries of the very man he meant to kill, who never sent him any warning at all, but took him unawares, and slew him, escaping by anticipation the fate that was in store for himself, without even knowing anything of all that this letter would have taught him, and so far from dying, living to a very great age. And this instance shows, that the most dangerous of enemies is the one that never threatens till he actually strikes, resembling not the cobra, but the adder, as Shatrunjaya discovered to his cost, too late.[7]

And the Daughter of the Snow exclaimed, in wrath: Why hast thou stopped, to tell me the end of the story, before even reaching the beginning?

And Maheshwara said: Aha! Snowy One, thou art not yet, as it seems, asleep. Many are the beginnings that never reach an end: but it will do this story no harm at all, to begin with the end, since all the essence of it lies in the middle, and as thou wilt find, it ends in the middle, and yet never ends, even when it is done.

What I have told thee does not matter in the least; what matters is the Queen, for she was the most extraordinary of all women, past, present, or to come.

And Párwatí said: Let the letter speak for itself: and if thou hast anything to say, keep it for the end. For nothing is more unendurable than a commentary upon a text which is unknown.

II

And Maheshwara said: Thus the letter continues:—for there is not room in one world for us both. And well thou knowest the reason why. For the Queen told me, the very last time that I saw her, that it would be the very last time, as indeed it was. And when I asked why she would see me no more, she said, that thine was the order, to send me away. Dog! was she thine to command, or was I? And yet, I knew very well, it was all thy doing, before ever she told me. For never would she have behaved as she did, had she not been pushed from behind: and the very first time that we met, when she told me of thee, I understood, and foresaw, and expected, the very thing that has happened, looking to find thee hiding behind her, to rid thee of a rival whom thou hadst not the courage openly to face. And dost thou dare to condemn me for doing the very same thing thou wast doing thyself? Was not my claim to love her as good as thy own? Or what, O cowardly dastard, does that man deserve, who screens himself behind the clothes of a woman to strike at a foe? I will answer the question, and show thee, by ocular proof, very soon. But now in the meantime, I will open thy eyes, and tell thee, from the very beginning, all that took place. And thou shalt learn how I stole her away from thee, in spite of thee, as presently I will come to rob thee also of thy life. And I will embitter thy life, and poison it, first: and then I will take it away.

III

And yet, strange indeed was the way that I met her. I cannot tell, whether it was a reward or a punishment for the deeds of a previous birth. For the joy of it would have been cheap, bought at the price of a hundred lives: and yet the sorrow is greater than the joy. And it happened thus. I was roaming through the world, with my lute for my only companion. For all men know, as thou must also, that I turned my back upon my hereditary kingdom, and quarrelled with all my relations, and left them, all for the sake of my lute. For ever since I was a child, I have cared for absolutely nothing but my lute, and as I think, I must have been a Gandharwa[8] in the birth before, since the sound of the tones of its strings, touched by the hand of a master musician, leads me like an ox that is pulled by a cord, the very moment I hear it, and I stand still, like one that listens with tears in his eyes to the memory of the voice of a friend that is dead. Ha! very wonderful are the influences of a forgotten birth! For I was an anomaly, behaving not according to my caste, which was that of a Rajpoot; and not music, but fighting, was my proper work, and my religion.[9] And it was as if my mother had been caught sleeping in the moonlight on the terrace of the palace in the hot season by some king of the Widyádharas passing by, and looking down from the air. For heavenly beings often fall into such temptations, and even an ascetic would have found it hard to laugh at the arrows of Manobhawa, coming in the form of such a feminine fascination as hers, lying still in the lunar ooze at midnight, with her head pillowed on her arm. And yet, for all my music, I was the tallest and strongest of all my clan, and a hunter, when I chose, that could bear fatigue even better than a Bhíl.

And then at last there came a day when the King my father sent for me. And when I came, he looked at me with approval, and he said: Thou art a man at last. And yet they tell me, thou dost nothing all day long but sit playing thy lute. Canst thou really be my son, or art thou some musician's brat, foisted into my son's place by some dark underhand intrigue, when I was looking the other way? For who ever heard of a Yuwarájá,[10] destined to sit upon the throne when I have entered the fire, neglecting all his duties for the sake of a lute's strings? Come now, throw thy lute away, and leave music to the professionals who have nothing else to do, and apply thyself to policy, and the things of a king's trade. And I said: What do I care for a kingdom in comparison with my lute? I will not throw it away, no, not for a hundred kingdoms. I am a devotee of Rádhá's lover,[11] and I care nothing for any ráj. Then my father flew into a rage. And he said: Thou shalt do, not as thou wilt, but as I will. Choose, between thy wretched lute, and the ráj: and if thou dost not obey, I will turn thee off, and put thy younger brother in thy place. And I said: There are kings in abundance everywhere, but those who can really play on a lute are very few indeed. And I am one. Let who will be a Yuwarájá: I will choose the lute. And he said, in wrath: Be off! and play dirges to the memory of thy dead succession, for thou art no longer heir. And I laughed in his face, and went away, and got on my horse, and turned my back upon it all, and rode off laughing with my lute hanging round my neck, counting the kingdom as a straw. And thereafter, I wandered up and down, from place to place, living as I pleased, and utterly disregarding the messages that reached me nearly every day from my mother, who sent me bags of money and entreaties to return, all in vain. And my story, like my playing, went from mouth to mouth, and everywhere I went, the people said: Ha! there goes Shatrunjaya, the mad musician, who cares more for a discord than the loss of his hereditary ráj! Ha! and if his policy were only equal to his playing, what a king he would have made! And what a fool he must be, to care for nothing in the three worlds but a lute's strings!

IV

And yet they were all wrong. For there was another thing that nobody knew anything about, that I cared for even more than for my lute. And all the while I wandered, I was looking for a thing that flew before me the more I kept pursuing it, like the setting of the sun. And yet it hung, so to say, always just before my eyes, like a picture on the wall, so that often I used to talk to it, as if it were alive, as I sat. And yet it never answered, looking back at me in silence with strange kind eyes, and seeming to listen to me gazing at it wistfully, and playing on my lute. And this was a woman, that had come to me in a dream. For but a little while before I quarrelled with my father, I was lying, on a day, at noon, when I had been following a quarry in the jungle till I ached with fatigue, resting on a river bank: and so as I lay, unawares I fell asleep. And I thought that I wandered through a palace that I had never seen before, till suddenly I came upon a terrace that stood on the very margin of a lake, that was filled with myriads of lotuses, all turned red by the rays of the setting sun, which stood never moving on the top of a low hill, as if it were watching me to see what I should do, before it went away. And there was such a strange silence that I began to be afraid, as if of something that was just about to happen, without knowing what. And so as we all stood waiting in the dusk, I and the lotuses and the sun, all at once I heard behind me a voice like a *kokila*, saying quietly: I have kept thee a long while waiting: wilt thou forgive?

And I turned round, and looked, and lo! there was a lady, looking at me with a smile. And she was standing so absolutely still, that she resembled an image made of copper, for exactly like the lotuses, she was all red in the rays of the sun, and her dark clothing shone like the leaf of a palm seen at midnight in the glow of a fire. And her hair was massed like that of an ascetic high over her brow, and on its dull black cloud there shone a gem that resembled a star, shooting and flickering and changing colour like a diamond mixed with an opal: while underneath, her eyes, that resembled pools filled with dusk instead of water, were fixed on me as if in meditation, as if half in doubt as to whether I was I. And yet her lips were smiling, not as if they meant to smile, but just because they could not help it, driven by the sweetness of the soul that lay behind them to betray its secret unawares. And the perfect oval of the outline of her face was lifted, so to say, into the superlative degree of soft fascination by a faint suggestion of the round ripeness of a fruit in its bloom, as if the Creator, by some magical extra touch of his chisel, had wished to exclaim: See how the full loveliness of a woman surpasses the delicate promise of a girl! And she was rather tall, and she stood up very straight indeed, so straight, that my heart laughed within me as I looked at her, for sheer delight, so admirably upright was the poise of her figure, and yet so round and delicious was the curve of her arms and her slender waist, that rose as if with exultation into the glorious magnificence of her splendid breast, on which her left hand rested, just touching it very lightly with the tips of her fingers, like a wind-blown leaf lying for a moment exactly at the point of junction of two mounds of snow, as if to chide it very gently for challenging the admiration of the three worlds. And she stood with her weight thrown on her left foot, so that her right hip, on which her right hand rested, swelled out in a huge curve that ran down to her knee, which was bent in, and then turned outwards, ending in a little foot that was standing very nearly on the tip of its toe.

And so as we stood, gazing at one another in dead silence, all at once she smiled outright, holding out both her hands. And at that very moment, the sun sank. And as I strove in vain to move, rooted to the spot like a tree, she faded away, very slowly, back again into the dark, growing little by little paler, till she vanished into the night, leaving nothing but her star, that seemed to glimmer at me from a great distance, low down on the very edge of a deep-red sky. And I strove and struggled in desperation to break the spell that held me chained, and suddenly I woke with a loud cry, and saw before me only the river, on whose bank I was lying alone.

V

Aye! then for the first time in my life, I knew what it meant, to be alone, which had been to me but a mere word, without any meaning at all. For as I sat by the river, I knew I had left my soul behind in the dream that had disappeared. And my heart was burning with such a pain that I could only breathe with great difficulty, and tears rose into my eyes, as it were of their own accord. And I said sadly to myself: Now, beyond all doubt, I have seen some feminine incarnation of a fallen star, and unless I can find it somewhere on earth, I shall lose the fruit of being born at all. So one thing only remains to do, and that is to look for her, and keep on looking until I find her. For if only I was sure, that she was absolutely beyond finding, I would not consent to remain in this miserable body without her, even for a single moment. But she must be alive somewhere, and able to be found: for how could such a thing as she was exist only in a dream? For nobody could possibly have invented her, no, not even in a dream: and it must be that my soul went roaming about as I slept, and actually caught sight of her. And if the soul could find her, then, she is somewhere to be found, even by the body; but alas! the body cannot travel so easily as the soul: since, in his haste, the Creator has forgotten to give wings to anything but birds. And yet, the only thing to do is to hunt for her incessantly, and go from place to place without stopping for a moment: since very certainly she will never be discovered if I remain here as motionless as a hill. So I must escape at once, on some pretence, without letting anybody know why.

And as I said, I did: and this was the very reason why I broke with my relations, and became a vagrant instead of a king's heir. And every night I went to sleep yearning to dream the dream again, and yet it never came, though even in my sleep I seemed in every dream to be roaming everlastingly in jungles, and along roads that never ended, always on the very point of finding something that I never found. And strange! instead of driving me to despair, this constant failure actually gave me courage, for I said: If the dream had really been only a dream and nothing more, it would surely have returned, beyond a doubt: since, as a rule, dreams are only pictures in the night of what men think of in the day. And yet she never comes again, although I think of nothing else, all day long, and she was very certainly no picture of anything that I ever saw before. And clearly, it must be that my soul did actually find her, though now it has lost its way, and does not know how to return.

And in the meanwhile, as time went on, the less I found her, the more I fell back upon my lute, which became the only confidante of my secret, and my sole refuge in my desolation. And I used to sit playing, thinking all the while of nothing but herself, so that she gradually became as it were the theme and the undertone of every air. And the listeners would say: Ha! now beyond a doubt this player on the lute must be some incarnation of a Kinnara, for the sound of his music resembles that of the wind singing in the hollows of the bamboos that wave over waterfalls on the sides of the snowy mountain: and his lute seems to sob, in the vain endeavour to express some melancholy secret that for want of words it cannot articulately tell, wringing as it were its hands of strings, for very grief: And I became a byword, and the fame of my music was carried into the quarters of the world, like the scent of the sandal that the breeze blows from the Malaya hill in the region of the South.

And then at last I came, on a day, tired out with travel, to Kamalapura.[12] And delighted with its trees and its river and its lotuses, I found a little house, and lodged in it, to rest for a while. And one morning, there came to me a musician of the city, who loved me for my playing, and he said: How comes it, O Shatrunjaya, that thou hast not been to play to Táráwalí?[13] And I said: Who is Táráwalí, that I should go to play to her, who never go to anyone at all? And he laughed, and exclaimed: Who is Táráwalí? What! dost thou actually say that thou hast never even heard of her, the Queen of this city? And I said: I did not know that thy Táráwalí was the same as the Queen, of whom indeed I have heard, very often, as everybody must who comes to this city: for as it seems, the citizens never talk of anything or anybody else, never saying anything about her that recommends her to me; since, as I understand, she is an independent[14] woman, who goes her own way, like the wind, caring absolutely nothing where it takes her, or what anybody says. And he said: Let them say what they will, at least she is a connoisseur in music, and plays the lute herself, though not so well as thou. And they tell me, she is very curious to see thee, and to hear thee, of whom she has heard so much. And I said carelessly: The curiosity is not reciprocal, since on my side there is absolutely none. And moreover, independent women are not to my taste, even when they happen to be queens. So it will be better for us both, to leave her curiosity unsatisfied. And he said: Well have they named thee, the mad musician: for thou art utterly unlike all other men. Thou hast thrown away thy kingdom for a lute: and now thou sittest like a stone, unmoved, to hear that even Táráwalí is curious on thy account: a thing that would set any other man dancing for delight, like a peacock at the sight of a cloud. Art thou indeed a stone, or is it sheer ignorance of what Táráwalí is like? And I said: And what then is she like? And he said: She is like absolutely nothing in the world but herself, and cannot therefore be described at all, but only seen. So the only way to get thy question answered is to go, and see her for thyself. And I said: Then it never will be answered, for I will not go and see. I am no tame animal, to go where I am called: I am wild. And he said: Aye! but the wild swans go to the Mánasa lake of their own accord. Thou art like a young wild swan, refusing, for sheer obstinacy, to visit the very place, that, had it only seen it, it would never be induced to desert again. For Táráwalí is exactly a Mánasa[15] for such a swan as thee. And for all answer, I took my lute, and began to pluck at the strings.

And he stood for a while, drumming on the sill of the window as he looked out: and then he turned and said: If thou hast no curiosity, thou hast at least the manners of a king's son. Wouldst thou be so uncivil as to say no to her invitation, if she sent to thee, to come? And I said: Why suppose what never can occur? Surely this independent queen does not go to such a length as to act like an *abhisáriká*,[16] and throw herself of her own accord at the head of every stranger that may wander through her city? And he laughed, and said: Wouldst thou actually shut thy door in her face, even so, if she were an incomparable beauty? Even an *abhisáriká* might be welcome, to anybody but thyself, who art said to be a hater of all women whatsoever. And I said: Why should I hate all women, who never think of them at all?

And he looked at me for a long while; and then he said: Who knows? Thou art so singular in everything that it is just barely possible that thou art telling me the truth, though it is very hard to believe it, in the mouth of a youth like thee. And yet, if as thou sayest, thy heart be really empty, Táráwalí could fill it for thee, easily enough. Aye! even if it were a desert equal to Marusthalí in dryness and extent, a single glance at her would turn it into an ocean, tossing with agitation, and running over with excess of salt.[17]

And then he went away. And instantly I forgot all about her, absorbed in my lute and the recollection of my dream.

VI

But next morning, when I awoke, his words all came back to me, and filled me with dismay. And I sat long musing over them, and saying to myself: Now after all, it is just possible not only that his words had a meaning, but even that he was acting as an agent of the Queen, who may take measures to make me go and see her, whether I will or no: since she is, as it seems, a musical blue-stocking,[18] ready to force herself on anybody just to gratify her vanity by claiming admiration for her musical proficiency, which nobody would acknowledge unless she were a queen. Out on these queens, that dabble in matters that they do not understand, and meddle in other people's business! But now I will steal a march on her by making my escape betimes, and I will go this very moment and order my horse to be got ready, to give her the slip, in case she may be meditating anything very disagreeable. For if she finds the bird flown, she will give it up, once for all.

And I went to the door and opened it, and lo! there in the street before me stood a woman, who was in the very act of knocking at the door, to get in, so that as I pulled it open, she very nearly fell into my arms. And as she drew back laughing, I looked at her in blank amazement. For she resembled a feminine incarnation of the dawn, being a very Apsaras for beauty, and very young, and very small, and dressed in a garment of red muslin, whose edge of gold ran all about her like a snake.[19] And she had gold bangles, and gold anklets, and gold chains about her neck, and she held the end of her garment drawn over her head with one hand, whose arm resembled a creeper spray, so that I could only just see her long eyes peeping at me through the opening. And I stood awhile, holding the door, and looking at her with dismay, that was very nearly terror, saying to myself: Now, after all, I am caught, for here she is in person, running to me of her own accord. And at last I said with hesitation: Art thou Tárávalí?

And instantly, that strange damsel broke into a peal of laughter. And she exclaimed: I, Táráwalí? Art thou stark mad? Or dost thou imagine Táráwalí would come to people's doors? Ha! then, but as it seems, thy thoughts are already running on Táráwalí. But let me come inside, for why should the whole street listen to our conversation? And she came in quickly and stood just inside the door, holding it by the handle, as if she wanted to make sure of her escape. And she said: Art thou Shatrunjaya, the lute-player? And I said: Yes. Then she said: Thou deservest almost to be slain, for such an extraordinary blunder as to confound such a thing as I am with the Queen. And yet, after all, thy chance arrow is somewhere near the mark: for if I am not Táráwalí, at least I am her shadow, and never very far from her, being her confidential maid. And I have come to thee now with a message from herself: and it is this: Táráwalí the pupil stands in sore need of Shatrunjaya the master, to help her in disentangling the quarter-tones of a theme: and she will await him in her garden, as the sun goes down.

And I said: What, O thou red beauty, is thy name? And she said: Chaturiká[20] Then I said: Go back, O Chaturiká, and tell the Queen that I was not to be found. I will not come. And here is gold for thee.

And Chaturiká brushed away my bribe with a wave of her pretty arm. And she leaned back against the door, holding the handle behind her, and looking up at me from under her long lashes, with sweet crafty eyes, and eyebrows lifted high into a double arch. And she put her head a little on one side, and said, with a smile: Think twice, O Shatrunjaya. Art thou a musician, and hast thou never heard the song: Nectar when she turns towards thee: poison when she turns away?[21] Or hast thou never tasted nectar, even in a dream? Remember, sunset! And she shook at me her forefinger, and suddenly she opened the door, and slipped out, and shut it, and was gone; leaving me staring at it in stupefaction, and almost believing I was dreaming, so abruptly had she come and gone. And I said to myself in wonder: Beyond a doubt, she spoke at random, knowing nothing of my dream; and yet she made me jump, for her arrow hit the mark exactly in the centre. But if the maid is like the mistress, of whom she said herself, she was the shadow, then very sure I am, it is not either maid or mistress, or anybody the least like them, that could realise my dream. But all the same, I am caught, for the moment, in their noose: and what is to be done now? For she will go straight back and tell it all, to this over-bearing busybody of a queen, and if now I do not go, it will seem an incivility almost equal to an insult. For queens do not like to be refused, and even their request is a kind of order, very difficult to disobey. Out, out, upon this red intrusive jade, and her mistress, and above all on myself, for my delay! For had I only gone away last night, I should have got clean off.

And long I sat debating, balanced in the swing of indecision, as to whether I should go, or not. And at last I exclaimed: I will give her just a chance. And I drew my *kattári* from its sheath, and I said: Now I will throw it into the air. And if it falls back upon its point, I will go and see her: but if not, not. And I threw it up, like a juggler, so that it spun very quickly like a wheel: and lo! it fell back, and stuck exactly on its point, standing straight up, as if on purpose to imitate Chaturiká's forefinger, and saying as it were: See! thou shalt go, willy nilly, at sunset to the Queen.

And so, seeing that I must absolutely go, I dismissed it, as a thing determined, from my mind. And a little before sunset, I went out, and moved slowly through the streets, making for the palace with unwilling feet. And when I reached it, I stood still, opposite the palace gates, saying to myself: There is still just time to turn back and go away. For my reluctance grew upon me as I went, with every step, as if some presentiment that I could not understand was warning me beforehand of all that would come about. And I said: Now then, I will give myself one last chance. I will stand here still, and count a hundred. And if in the time, I do not see an elephant go by, I will go away, bidding good-bye for ever to the Queen. And then I began to count. And strange! at that very moment, I looked, and saw the *ankusha* of a *mahávat*, high up above the crowd, coming round the corner. And the elephant on which he sat passed by the palace gates, looking at me as it were with laughter in its little eye, and saying: I am just in time: while yet I had fifty still to count.

So near I came, to never seeing Tárávalí at all!

VII

So then at last, seeing that fate was against me, and that there was absolutely no help for it, I gave up the struggle, and went up to the gate. And learning who I was, the *pratihárí*[22] led me away into the palace, and I followed her through innumerable corridors and halls, until at last we came to a high wall, in which there was a door, screened by a curtain. And she drew aside the curtain, and opened the door with a key. And she said: The Queen is within: knock at the door on thy return. And I went in, and she shut the door behind me, leaving me alone.

And I found myself in a garden, of which I could not see the end, for it rather resembled a forest for its multitude of trees. And after a while, I went on slowly without any guide, going wherever my steps led me, and saying to myself as I went along: Now I wonder where the Queen is; for as it seems, I am far more likely to lose myself than find anything, in such a maze as this. And then, little by little, I utterly forgot all about her, lost in my admiration of the place that I was in, and saying to myself in wonder: After all, I did well to come, and it was well worth while, if only for the sake of this extraordinary wood, which cannot properly be called a garden, since it is like absolutely nothing else in the world. For there were no flowers to be seen at all, but only trees. And even of trees, there were only four kinds, champak, and *shála*, and *nyagrodha*, and bamboo. But every kind of tree was multiplied many times, and each was a very giant, and a marvel of its kind. And the champaks and the *shálas* were loaded with their blossoms that filled the air with heavy fragrance, and glimmered in the dusk: and the bamboos stood in clumps, like pillars, each as thick as my own body, with their tall plumes waving very gently to and fro like *chowris* over my head; and the trunks and the roots of the *nyagrodhas*[23] writhed and twisted round me like serpents' coils and women's limbs, pointing at me as it were with weird wooden arms, till I felt as if I were walking in some strange dream forest whose Yakshas and Yakshinís were watching me and mocking me as I went along. And suddenly, I looked, and far away through the trees I saw the moon nearly full rising slowly like a great red nocturnal sun, on the edge of the pallid eastern sky, as if it had come to watch me too, before the sun was down. And a feeling that was almost fear began to creep into my soul, as I moved on slowly, not knowing where I was. And all at once, I came out suddenly upon a terrace and stood still. For just below me was a lake, whose water was black, and absolutely still, and it was filled with innumerable lotuses, that stood straight up out of the mirror that they floated in, all turned red by the rays of the setting sun, which was just about to disappear, taking as it were a last fond look at them, as it stood, blood-red, on the rim of the world.

And then, like a flash of lightning, recollection rushed into my soul. And my heart gave a bound, as if it wanted to leap from my body. And I exclaimed, with agitation: Ha! Why, it is the very lake, and these are the very lotuses, and the very sun that I saw in my dream! And even as I spoke, I heard behind me the low sweet voice of a woman, saying slowly: I fear that I have kept thee waiting for a long time: and canst thou forgive me?

And instantly I cried out: The words! the words! And I turned sharp round, shaking like a leaf, with a heart that beat in my body like a drum. Lo! there, just before me, stood the lady of my dream. And exactly as before, her dark blue garments shone like copper in the red sun's rays, and the star stood trembling in her high dark hair. And exactly as before, she stood up, absolutely straight, as if on purpose to throw into strong relief the undulating curves of her lovely form, and yet she differed from her own dream in this, that her soft round bosom was rising and falling like an agitated wave, as if she had been running very fast with nimble feet, that had stopped short, at the sight of me. And she held her pretty head, with appealing grace, just a very little on one side, looking at me with great sweet eyes, and lips that smiled, half-open, as if to let her breathe, saying as it were: I know that I am very guilty, and yet I am absolutely sure to be forgiven, since you cannot find it in your heart to scold. And somehow or other, there came from every part of her as it were the delicious fragrance of an extreme desire to oblige and please, that exactly corresponded with the excessive gentleness of the voice that had just spoken; and yet it was mixed in some inexplicable way with a very faint suggestion of authority, as though to say: All will willingly obey me; but those who will not, must. And one hand hung down by her side, holding a lute by a yellow string: while the other was playing with the beads of a necklace of great pearls, that lay on the ocean of her surging breast, so that it was carried up and down on its wave. And she looked, as she stood before me, like a faultless feminine incarnation of the essence of a bosom friend, turned into an instrument of supernatural seduction by the infusion of the intoxication of the other sex, and seeming as it were to say: How much dearer is a dear friend, that looks at thee with a woman's eyes!

And I stood for a single instant, looking, with a soul that struggled to leave me, as if it had recognised at once, the moment it caught sight of her, whose claim it should obey. And I made a step towards her, stretching out both my hands: and all at once, I uttered a sharp cry, and fell at her feet in a swoon.

VIII

And when I came back to myself, I opened my eyes, and saw her, standing close beside me, bending over towards me, and watching me with eyes that were full of an expression that was half anxiety and half compassion. And as I rose to my feet, in confusion, she said quietly: Nay, it would be better for thee to sit still, for a little while, until thou art recovered. Art thou ill, or what is the matter with thee? And I looked at her, making as it were sure of her being really there, and I said with emotion: Nay, on the contrary, I am very well indeed, now that I find thee still here, as I never hoped to see thee. For I was terribly afraid, lest I should lose thee as I did before. And the shock was like a blow, for I have waited so long, to see thee again. And she looked at me with astonishment, and she said: Before? Again? What dost thou mean? When have we ever met before? And I said: In a dream. And it may be, even earlier, in some former birth. I cannot tell. But instantly, I knew thee again, and my heart stopped, unable to endure the unutterable joy, and the choking pain, and the suddenness of the surprise: for it came upon me like a thunderbolt, without warning. And as I said, I was white with terror, lest thou shouldst have taken advantage of my swoon, to disappear, as thou didst before. For if I had not seen thee, when I woke up, I should have died.

And she looked at me for a while, with curiosity, and as if meditating over what I said. And then she sighed. And she said in a low voice, as if speaking to herself: This is my fault. Alas! I foresaw that there would be danger in thy coming. And I exclaimed: Danger! Be under no concern. Thou hast nothing at all to fear from me, or indeed from anything whatever, as long as I am near thee. Then she said: Nay, but thou dost not understand. It is not for myself that I was afraid, but for thee. And as I looked at her, as if to ask her what she meant, she said again: It is I who am the danger. For I know by experience that I always act on thy sex like a spell: only in thy case, the spell was very strong: so strong, as almost to destroy thee. And yet, it is not my fault, after all. Blame me not, but rather blame the Creator who made me as I am. And I exclaimed: Blame him! nay, rather worship and adore him, for the wonder of his work: as thou art very certainly his masterpiece. What! wouldst thou have me blame him, for producing a thing that I could worship, instead of himself? And she shook her head slowly as I spoke, and she said: Thou seest: it is exactly as I said. I am a poison to thee. And I looked at her, trembling with sheer ecstasy to look at her and listen to her: and suddenly I burst out laughing, with my eyes full of tears. And I said: Poison! Thou! Ah! let me only drink such poison to its dregs! I ask for nothing more. And she said: Come! let us sit on the step, and thou wilt recover. And when we were seated, she said, after a while: Forget me, if thou canst, for a moment, and listen, and I will tell thee of the difficulty which led me to summon thee to my assistance.

And then she began to speak to me of the musical intervals, while I sat gazing at her, drunk with admiration, and growing hot and cold by turns, never so much as hearing a single word she said, but listening only to the unutterable sweetness of the voice that spoke, that sounded in my ears like the noise of a waterfall coming from a distance to the ear of one that lies dying of thirst. And all at once, I broke in abruptly, without any reference whatever to her words: and I said: O Táráwalí, they named thee well who chose thy name: for thou art indeed like the star on thy brow. And when I think how nearly I never came to thee at all, I shudder for sheer terror, to think I all but missed my opportunity, and lost thee for ever. And I owe thee an apology, for a crime, done to thy divinity in ignorance. Aye! Chaturiká was right, when she told me I was worthy of death, for confounding thee with her.

And she said, with a sigh: Thou art not listening to what I say. And then she smiled, with a little smile that shook my heart for delight, and she said: Aye! Chaturiká told me of thy error. But trust her not, when she speaks of me, for she is a flatterer. And yet, thy crime was venial, and one easily forgiven: for she is very pretty, as I am not. But we are wandering from the point, and wasting time, and talking nonsense. Forget us both, and listen with attention, and I will begin all over again. And I swept away her beginning with a wave of my hand, and I exclaimed: It is useless, for I can listen at present to absolutely nothing. There is no room in my soul for anything but thee. Speak to me of thyself, and I will listen never moving for the remainder of my life. And once again she sighed, lifting her hands, and letting them fall again, as if in despair. And she said gently: If thou absolutely wilt not attend, where was the use of thy coming at all? And I said: If thou wilt only send for me every day, at sunset, for a year, it may be that I shall at last be able to forget thee sufficiently, for a very little while, to attend to something else.

And suddenly she laughed, with laughter that exactly resembled the laughter of a child, and she said: Thou art very crafty indeed, but thy cunning plan would take a long time, with but little result. And even then, I am not sure I could rely on thy forgetting. And I exclaimed, with emphasis: Thou art absolutely right, for the moment of oblivion would never come at all. But O thou miracle of a queen, tell me at least one thing about thyself. And she said: What? And I said: How can the King thy husband be so utterly bereft of his reason as to let any other man see his star? Or is he, in very truth, actually blind? For I could understand it, if he really cannot see.

And she looked at me with surprise: and she said slowly: Dost thou actually not know, what everybody knows? And I said: I know nothing that everybody knows, being as I am a stranger. But this I know, very well, that if thou wert *my* pearl, I would take very good care to hide thee. For even an honest man might well turn robber, tempted by the sight of such an ocean pearl. And she said, very quietly: It needs no thief to steal the pearl, if indeed it be a pearl, which its owner cast away long ago as a thing of no value, for anyone to pick up as he passes by.

And I stared at her in stupefaction, and I struck my hands together and exclaimed: Art thou mad, or am I dreaming? And she said gently: It is true. And anybody but a stranger like thyself would have known it, without needing to be told. And she dropped her eyes, and sat for a while, fingering the string of her lute, as if on purpose to make herself into a picture for my intoxicated gaze: and suddenly she said: Why should I make a secret of a thing that another will tell thee, if I do not, adding to the truth slanders that are false? It is better for thee, and for me, to learn from my own mouth what it is impossible to hide. There is a relation of the King, whose name is Narasinha. And one day he saw me by accident, on the roof of the palace, and instantly he lost his reason, as all the men who see me always do. And not long after, the King was set upon by numbers in a battle, and within a very little of being slain; and Narasinha saved his life, very nearly losing his own. And the King said, when all was over: Now, then, O Narasinha, ask me for anything I have, no matter what: it is thine. And Narasinha saw his opportunity. And he shut his eyes, like one that leaps from a precipice to life or death. And he said: Give me thy Queen, Táráwalí: or else, slay me, here and now, with this very sword that saved thy life. And then, to his amazement, as he stood with his head bowed, expecting death, the King burst out laughing. And he said: Is that all? Aha! Narasinha, we were both frightened, thou and I: thou, of asking, and I, of what thou mightest ask. Didst thou not think, I should slay thee, for thinking of her even in a dream? But my life were worth little, if I haggled with its saviour over its price. And Táráwalí is thine, to do with as thou wilt. For I have only one life, whereas queens can be found in all directions, and I can very easily replace her, whenever I choose. Only she must not leave the palace, for after all, she is my Queen, and so she must remain, for everyone but me and thee. And so he gave me clean away to Narasinha, in secret, but it is a secret that everybody knows, and tells in secret to everybody else. And I have gained by the exchange. For Narasinha risked his life, twice, to win me, and the King would never have risked so much as his little finger to save the life of a hundred queens, and gave me away, like a straw, for the mere asking, not even stopping to consider, that in the straw he gave away his own honour lay hidden, which he gave away with me. And I could have forgiven him for giving me away, but who could forgive the King who valued his own honour less than his own life? And to the King I was never more than a necessary ornament, a thing like a sceptre and a throne, and a mere piece of royal furniture: whereas I am more than the life of Narasinha, and the apple of his eye.

IX

And as she spoke, I listened, not believing my own ears, and saying to myself: Is it all real, or can it be that I am only dreaming after all? And which is the greater wonder, this miserable King, who, leaving honour out of the account, is so utterly besotted as to give away a thing like her to the first man who asks for her, or Táráwalí herself, telling the whole story of her own depreciation with such contemptuous and yet delicious candour to such a one as me? Aye! well indeed she might despise a husband so unutterably despicable; and yet his oblivion of his own honour is easier by far to understand than his blindness to the value of the thing he gave away. And would she tell me anything at all, unless she had come to the conclusion that I was worthy of her confidence? And who knows? For why should she consent to be given like a horse to Narasinha? Why might she not prefer to give herself, and choose for herself the man who was to be her owner? And what if I could persuade her to let me be the man? And at the very thought, my head began to swim in the delirium of hope and almost unimaginable anticipation. And I said: Dear Táráwalí, is it the fault of the ocean gem, if its boorish owner flings it away, taking it for a bit of common glass, and ignoring its inestimable worth? There are other and better judges, who would give their very lives, only to be allowed to pick it up.

And she looked at me with a smile, and she leaned towards me, and she said, with gentle mischief in her eyes: Shall I tell thee thy very thoughts, and it may be, tumble down for thee the unsubstantial castles thou art even already building in the air? Thou art marvelling at the King, for giving me so carelessly away: and thou art wondering, why I am telling thee about it: and last of all, it may be, thou art counting on my independence. Is it not so? And I hung my head in silence, ashamed at being so accurately detected by the subtle penetration of this extraordinary Queen. And presently she said, as if to console me for my confusion, with unutterable sweetness in her voice: Come, do not allow delusive imagination to run away with thee, but curb him, and rein him up, and stop him, and be wise. For I belong, body and soul, to Narasinha. And yet, for all that, I am my own mistress, and act exactly as I choose. And I see anyone I please, and at my own time, and go, like a wild elephant, wherever inclination leads me. And music is my passion, and I heard of thee, and sent for thee, and now that I have seen thee, I like thee. And now, shall we be friends?

And as she ended, she put out towards me both her hands, leaning towards me, and looking at me with a smile, and eyes full of an invitation so irresistibly caressing that it swept away my self-control, consuming it like a blade of grass in a forest fire. And I started to my feet, and instantly she rose herself. And I seized her right hand in my own, with a grip that made it an unwilling prisoner beyond all hope of escape. And I exclaimed with agitation: Friends! only friends! Alas! O Táráwalí, hast thou given thyself, body and soul, so absolutely to Narasinha, as not to have left even the very smallest atom over, for me, now that I have discovered thee at last? O I have dreamed of thee, and thy sweetness, and thy eyes, so long, so long.

And as I gazed at her, forgetting everything in the world, but my incontrollable thirst for herself, she sighed, and she said with compassion: Poor boy! I did ill, to summon thee at all. Thou art only drinking poison, and yet I know not any antidote, save only to bid thee go away.

And I stood, bereft of my senses, and without knowing what I did, pulling her by the hand, that lay reluctantly in mine, endeavouring to free itself in vain. And half resisting, half consenting, against her own will, to be pulled, she came slowly towards me, leaning back, and looking at me with eyes that seemed to implore me to release her, and yet, unable to be harsh, no matter what I did. And at last, she reached me, and she closed her eyes, as I kissed her, with a shudder of delight that was almost terror, on the lips. And then instantly I let her go, and stood aghast at what I had done. And I stammered: Forgive! for I did not know what I was doing.

And she shook her head, and said very gently: Nay, it is I myself who am to blame: since I might have known that this would be the inevitable end. But now, good-bye! for thou hast been here already far too long. And then, she hesitated for an instant, looking at me as if with pity; and she said with a smile: Thou must absolutely go, and yet my heart is sorry for thee, for I understand, what going means, to thee. Come, if thou wilt, I will allow thee, to bid me good-bye.

And as she held out her arms, looking at me with a smile, my reason fled. And I caught her anyhow, with one arm round her waist, and the other round her neck, turning round unawares, so that suddenly I found her lying in my arms, gazing up into my eyes, with lips that trembled as they smiled. And I drew a deep sigh, and then I kissed her in a frenzy with a kiss that seemed as if it would never end.

And then, I almost threw her from me, with a cry. And I turned and fled away, without looking back, and found, I know not how, the door, and knocked, and it was opened; and I got, somehow or other, into the street. And I went home like one walking in a dream, with feet that found their way of their own accord.

X

And I threw myself on my bed, and lay, all night long, asleep or awake, I know not which, but gazing with eyes that as it were shone into the dark, and a heart burning with the fire of joy, and a soul lost in the ecstasy of recollection, saying to myself without ceasing: I have found her, I have found her: and the reality is sweeter far even than the dream. And morning arrived, as it seemed, even before night had begun, for time was lost altogether in the abyss of reminiscence. And I rose up, and stood still, with my eyes fixed upon the ground, going over every detail, and striving to recall every atom of the meeting of the day before. And I said to myself: Ha! and fool that I was, I very nearly missed her, by refusing to go at all. And unless that lucky elephant had chanced to come along, I was absolutely lost. And yet, how could I possibly have guessed that Táráwalí would turn out to be the lady of my dream? O joy, that she caught me just before I went away! O the star in her hair, and the sound of her voice, and O the unendurable torture of being absent for an instant from the possibility of the nectar of her kiss!

And then, all at once, I started, for a thought ran of its own accord like a dagger straight into my heart. And I exclaimed: Alas! I had forgotten. How in the world am I ever to see her again? And she said: Good-bye! Can it be that she intended I was never to return? Alas! beyond a doubt, good-bye was good-bye, and for all her extraordinary kindness, she was offended by my overweening presumption, and sent me away, and will not send for me again. Aye! all is over: for like Durgá,[24] she is absolutely inaccessible, unless she chooses to reveal herself to her miserable devotee of her own accord. Aye indeed! my arrogance has ruined me in her estimation, and I cannot even hope ever to see her any more. Fool that I was, and mad, to run away like a deer, never so much as dreaming of providing for my return! Now indeed, I have dropped myself into a well without a rope, and she is as utterly beyond my reach, as if indeed she were a star.

And my knees shook, and I sank down, with my head buried in my hands, ready to cry, for sheer anguish, at the thought of my inability to get at her, and the horror on purpose to keep me in suspense, and torture my impatience. And then at last, she said: Sunset! What! didst thou fear I was going to say Farewell?

And as she laughed again, I caught her by the hand, in exultation, and her laughter suddenly changed into a shriek. And she said, with more laughter: Nay, thou hast come within a little of breaking my hand in pieces, gripping it like one that catches at a twig, to save himself from drowning. What! wouldst thou requite a benefit, by injuring thy benefactor? Or hast thou again mistaken one hand for another? And again she began to laugh, looking at me slily, with her provoking pretty eyes: and she said: No matter, I forgive thee, for as I said, I understand. But O Shatrunjaya the lute-player, what is it that has made thee change thy mind, since yesterday? Or am I to go back and tell the Queen, once more, that her music-master will not come?

And she turned, laughing still, to go away. But I sprang forward, and caught her in my arms again, and said: Nay, dear Chaturiká, do not go. Stay just a little longer, for art thou not her shadow?

And yet once more she began to laugh, pushing me away, as she exclaimed: It is utterly impossible, O Shatrunjaya, for I have many things to do, and very little time. And I am not sure that I care to be embraced, merely because I am the shadow of another. Thou must contrive how thou canst, without me, to restrain thy insatiable appetite of embracing other people, till sunset. Patience! thou hast not long to wait.

And she went out and shut the door, and suddenly, just as it was closing, she opened it again, and put in her head. And she said: Shall I tell her of thy anxiety to embrace me, or leave it to thee? Dear Chaturiká! Ah! ah! Nectar when she turns towards thee: poison when she turns away!

And then she shut the door and disappeared.

XI

And as the door shut behind her, she left the whole room filled to the very brim with the red glow of triumphant love's emotion, and the atmosphere of the ecstasy of happiness; and the laughter, of which she seemed to be the incarnation, hung, so to say, in every corner of the room. And my heart sang and my blood bubbled with the wave of the ocean of anticipation that surged and swelled within me, so that I was utterly unable to sit still, for sheer joy; and my soul began as it were to dance in such excitement, that I could hardly refrain from shouting, resembling one intoxicated by the abruptness of a sudden change from certain death to the very apex of life's sweetness. And I said to myself: Sunset! So, then, beyond a doubt, she has either forgiven me, or is willing to forgive. And who knows? For if she has forgiven once, she may forgive again: when again, it may be, she will allow me to say good-bye. And at the thought, my heart began to burn with dull fire, hurting me so that I could hardly breathe: and yet strange! the pain was divided only by a hair from a sweetness so intense that I laughed aloud, without knowing why, like one hovering on the very verge of being mad. And so I remained, drowned in the ocean of the torture and the nectar of love-longing, every now and then waking as from a day-dream to wonder at the sun, who seemed to dawdle on his way, as if on purpose to separate my soul from my body with impatience. But at last, after all, day began slowly to come to an end, and I set out for the palace, with feet that could hardly be restrained from running as fast as they could go.

And at the gate the very same *pratihárí* was waiting, and she led me away, exactly as before, to the door, and opened it, and I went in. And I stood, listening to its sound as it shut behind me, hardly able to believe that it was not a dream, as I found myself once more in the garden that contained the Queen. And I stopped for a while, for my heart was beating so furiously that I was afraid it would break. And I said to myself, with a sigh of ineffable relief: Ah! now, then, I am actually here, once more. And O now, very soon, comes the agonising rapture of seeing her again. And I wonder where she is, and how I shall find her to-night. And now I must begin to hunt for a very sweet quarry. And suddenly I started almost running, paying absolutely no attention to the trees at all, with eyes that were blind for everything in the world, except one.

And then, all at once, I stopped short: for I looked and saw her, a little way off, under a great *nyagrodha* tree, sitting crossways in a low swing[25] that hung down from a long bough, holding one of its ropes in her left hand that was stretched as high as it could go, and leaning back against the other with her head cushioned in her bent right arm. And she had her left foot tucked beneath her, so that her left knee stood up in the swing, while her right leg was stretched out below, so that its foot just reached the ground, to allow her to swing very gently, whenever her toes touched the earth. And the lovely line of her great right hip seemed to cry for admiration, running down in a single unbroken curve from her waist into the ground, balanced as it were above by the slender beauty of her left arm rising from the mound of her left breast. And the rising moon which she was watching touched her with a faint lustre, lighting up like a lamp the great gem in her hair, and making the champak blossom that floated in the hollow of her bosom's wave glimmer like the foam on a midnight sea. And after a while, I began to steal towards her on tiptoe, fearing to disturb her, lest the lovely picture should be spoiled, yet yearning to be with her with the whole strength of my soul. But all at once, she heard me coming, and looked round and saw me. And instantly she left her swing, and came towards me, walking quickly with undulating steps, as upright as a pillar of her own tree. And I stood still, to watch her coming, and adore it, and delay it, but she reached me in a moment, and she stopped, and said with a smile: I am very glad to see thee. I sent thee, by the mouth of Chaturiká, a time, and yet I hardly dared to hope for thy coming: since doubtless thou hast a better use for thy hours than to waste them upon me.

And I stared at her, in utter stupefaction: and then, all at once I began to laugh. And I exclaimed: Waste! I do not understand. What dost thou mean? Or what was thy object in bidding me to come to thee at sunset? Surely not merely to talk to me of music? And she looked at me gently, with surprise. And she said: Of course. What other object could I have? And I looked at her in silence, saying to myself: Can it really be possible that she means exactly what she says, and that this was the only significance of the word she sent to me? And suddenly I leaned towards her, with hunger in my eyes. And I said: Then indeed, I was mistaken. It was not so, that I interpreted thy summons. Alas! O Táráwalí, the only music that I came for was the music of thy incomparable voice, and I thought it was thy own deliberate intention to send for me simply that I might listen to it again, as I gazed on its owner with adoration.

And she looked at me reproachfully, and she said: Again! Alas! I imagined that thou wouldst ere now have recovered from thy shock of yesterday, and be able now to help me; and yet, here is thy delusion returning, as it seems, even worse than before. See now, forget altogether that I am a woman, and let us talk of music, like two friends. And I laughed in derision, and I exclaimed: Forget that thou art a woman! Ask me rather to forget I am a man. Art thou blind, or hast thou never even looked into a mirror? Dost thou imagine me less than a man, bidding me forget that she is a woman who stands before me, as thou dost, smiling, and bewildering my soul with her maddening loveliness, and the absolute perfection of her body and her soul, showing the hungry man food, and forbidding him to eat, and the thirsty man water, and requiring him to think of it as something it is not? Or art thou all the time only playing, having no heart in thy body, or a stone for a heart? Didst thou summon me only to torture and torment me? Dost thou not know, canst thou not see, the agony of my suffering, standing close enough to seize thee in my arms, and yet kept at a distance, to listen to what I cannot even understand? I tell thee, I am drunk with thy beauty, and mad with intolerable desire for the incomprehensible fascination of thy charm, and dost thou dream of quenching my fire by talking about friends? I want no friendship from thee. I will be more than a friend to thee, or less: aye! I would give all the friendship in the three worlds for a single drop of nectar, mixed of thy body and thy soul.

And as I spoke, she listened, putting up every now and then her hand, as if to stop me: and when I ended, she stood, looking at me in perplexity, as if utterly unable to decide what to do. And at last, I said: Why dost thou say nothing? And she said, simply; I do not know what to say. And I laughed aloud, lost in admiration of the extraordinary simplicity of her incomparable reply. And I exclaimed: O thou wonderful woman, how can I find words to express what I feel for thee? And she said, as if with despair: I counted on thy recovery. And I said: Count not on my recovery, for I never shall recover. And she said, with a smile: Then, as it seems, I shall never have my music lesson. And perhaps it would be better, if it ended here, without ever having begun. And in any case, to-night, thy visit must of necessity be a very short one, since I have other business, unexpectedly arisen, to do. And so, shall we say good-night, without any more delay?

And I said slowly: If I must go, I must: for I will obey thee, order what thou wilt. And yet, wilt thou not allow me at least to bid thee good-bye, as thou didst last night?

And she looked at me, as I leaned towards her, as if with reproach, and she stood for a moment, hesitating, and as it were, balanced in the swing of her own beautiful irresolution. And then, after a while, she sighed, and put out her hand, as if with resignation. And I drew her to me with a clutch, and caught her in my arms, showering on her lips and her eyes and her hair kisses that resembled a rain of fire: while all the time she offered absolutely no resistance, allowing me to do with her exactly as I pleased. And when at last I stopped to breathe, looking at her with eyes dim with emotion, she said, very gently, with a smile, lying just as she was, fettered in my arms: Hast thou yet bid me good-bye, to thy satisfaction? And I said in a low voice: Nay, not at all. For thou hast not yet kissed me in return, even once. And as if out of compassion, she did as she was told: kissing me gently, over and over again, for I would not let her stop, with kisses that resembled snowflakes that burned as they fell.

And at last, I let her go. And holding her two hands, I gazed at her for a while in adoration, while she looked at me as if patiently waiting to be released, with a little smile. And I said: Now then I will obey thee, and go: for thou hast given me something that will keep me alive. And yet thou art cheating me by sending me away before the time, and thou owest me the rest. Promise me, that thou wilt summon me to-morrow, or I cannot go away, even if I try. For if I go, not knowing when I shall see thee again, I will slay myself on thy palace steps.

And she drew away her hands, very gently, and turned away, and stood looking down upon the ground, reflecting. And I watched her, as I waited, with anxiety: for she seemed to be meditating, not so much of me, as of something unknown to me, that stood in the way of her decision. And then at last, she turned towards me, looking at me, as it seemed, with pity. And she said, almost sadly, and yet with a smile: Poor moth, thou wilt only burn away thy wings. Thou little knowest, what eyes are on thee, or the danger thou art running by overestimating me, and coming here at all. And yet, the mischief has been done, and thou art greatly to be pitied, having fallen under a spell: and thou art suffering from a fever to which nothing can bring any alleviation but myself. And it would be far better to refuse thee, since to grant thy request cannot possibly do thee any good. And yet I cannot find it in my heart to deny thee what thou cravest, since I am myself the involuntary cause of all thy delusion, and can give thee such extraordinary pleasure, with so very little trouble to myself. And so, I will give thee thy desire, and to-morrow's sunset shall be thine.

And I uttered a cry of joy. And utterly unable to control my emotion, I caught her once more in my arms, kissing her passionately with trembling lips. And suddenly I shuddered with delight, for I felt her lips kissing me again. And my senses reeled, and I murmured with emotion: Ah! thou lady of my dream, art thou real, or am I still only dreaming after all? And she stood back, putting me away with her hand, and she said, gently: I am real, but thou seest me through the eyes of thy dream. For what is there, after all, in me, save what thou puttest there thyself, with the aid of thy fancy, and thy passion, and the recollection of thy dream?

And I looked at her in silence for a while, and then I said: Promise me yet one thing more. And she smiled, and said: Thou art insatiable: and yet, what is it? And I said: Send me Chaturiká in the morning, just to tell me what I know already. For I shall be dying of impatience, and she is like a foretaste of thyself, and will help to keep me alive.

And she laughed, and she said: Ah! thou art very crafty, for Chaturiká is far prettier than I. But I will send her for all that, to gratify thee to the full. And moreover, I am not jealous. But now, thou must absolutely go: for I must also. And she leaned towards me, with eyes that were full of an unutterable caress: and she said: To-morrow, at sunset, I will be thy dream. Only remember, not to blame me, for anything that may happen when awaking comes.

And I turned and went away, with a heart that trembled in the extremity of joy. And when I had gone a little way, I looked back, and saw her still standing, looking after me, with her two hands clasped behind her head, as motionless as a tree. And after a little while, I looked again, and she was gone.

XII

And when I got home, I threw myself on my bed, and instantly fell fast asleep, for I was worn out by emotion and fatigue: and my slumber resembled the deep peace of my own heart. And a little before the dawn, I woke up, and went out, wandering where my footsteps led me, with a soul lost in meditation on Táráwalí, bathed in the nectar of reminiscence and anticipation, and yet puzzled by a doubt that it could not resolve. And I said to myself as I went along: How in the world can a queen like her, who laughs all other women to utter scorn, for beauty and understanding and gentleness and sweetness, and some unintelligible magic charm that is somehow spread all over her, and echoes in the tone of her delicious voice that makes every fibre of my heart tremble every time I hear it; how can such a queen as she show such extraordinary favour to such a thing as me? For I could understand it, if it were any other man. For then I should say that beyond all doubt, she actually preferred him to all others in the world, for sheer affection. And yet, as it is, it is quite incomprehensible. For, it might seem, that she must be in love with me herself, returning my affection: and yet it cannot be. For how could such a miracle as she is, the supreme achievement of the Creator, and the concentrated essence of the charm of all her sex, think of such a one as me, even in a dream, as an object of affection? And yet, if not, how is her behaviour to be explained? For I might perhaps believe that she was merely playing with me for her own amusement, were she any other woman than exactly the one she is: but as it is, no one could believe it that had ever seen her for an instant: and she needs no other argument in her defence than every glance at her supplies. And it may be, after all, that she took up with Narasinha merely out of pique, at being so unceremoniously slighted and cast off as a thing of no value by her booby of a husband, and, as it were, also out of gratitude to find herself appreciated at her true value, which she must very well understand notwithstanding all her own beautiful self-depreciation, which is an extra charm enhancing all her other charms: and afterwards, it may be, she has changed her mind, as women do, about Narasinha, without being willing to admit it, even to herself; and come, only the other day, suddenly on me. Aye! beyond a doubt, this would be the true conclusion, and the answer to the riddle, but for one consideration that makes it utterly impossible, that I am only I.

And so as I debated with myself, all at once I heard my own name called aloud in the air. And I looked up, and lo! there was my old friend Haridása,[26] on a camel. And he said: Ha! Shatrunjaya, art thou thyself indeed, or another exactly like thee, or hast thou lost thy senses and thy ears? For here have I been calling to thee, all along the street, without succeeding in waking thee from thy dream, till now. And what can it be, that can so fill thy mind as to stop up all its entrances?

And I exclaimed in delight: Ah! Haridása, thou art come in the very nick of time, the very man, at this moment, that I need most. Get off thy camel, for a while, and come and sit beside me, and find me, if thou canst, an answer to a question that I cannot find myself. And so he did. And as soon as we were seated by the roadside, I said to him: Haridása, listen. Thou knowest me well. Now tell me thy opinion: am I one that a woman might choose out of many for a lover?

And Haridása began to laugh. And he looked at me shrewdly, and he said: Aha! Shatrunjaya the lute-player, so this was thy preoccupation? Art thou one to catch a woman's fancy? O Shatrunjaya, why not? For art thou not a musician, famous in the world, and a man among men, into the bargain? All women love a giant, such as thou art. Any woman of them all might do worse than fall in love with thee. And yet thy very question shows, that in this matter of women, thou art little better than a child, as indeed thou always wert. For even the Deity himself can never tell what man any woman will prefer, or why: as how should he, seeing that she does not even know, herself? And there never yet existed any man whom some woman would not worship, let him be as ugly as you please, or even for that very reason: and yet, let a man be a very Kámadewa, woman after woman will pass him by, without even so much as casting a glance at him out of the very corner of her eye. For a woman's affection depends on her fancy, and that is like the wind, that comes and goes and wavers how and where it will, without a reason that anybody can discover. And it is sheer waste of time to sit and wonder, whether thou art or art not a man that a woman might love. Thou art both, or neither: for the only way to settle thy question is to try. And she will, or she will not, of her own accord. And now, who is she, this beauty who has set thee so knotty a problem to solve?

And I said with indifference: There is no such beauty; for all my perplexity arose from the line of an old song: Nectar when she turns towards thee: poison when she turns away.

And Haridása turned sharp towards me, and looked at me intently for a very long while, saying absolutely nothing. And we sat talking of other things till he rose to go away. And then, at the very moment he was mounting on his camel, he turned, and came back. And he said: Listen!

Thou art hiding from me something that maybe I could startle thee by guessing: but no matter. Keep thy secret: but listen to a piece of good advice, which may serve thee at a pinch. If ever thou wouldst have a woman prize thee, never let her see that thou settest any store by her. Treat her as a straw, and she will run after thee as if thou wert a magnet: make thyself her slave, and she will hold thee cheap, and discard thee for another. For women think meanly of their sex, and utterly despise the man who places them above himself: since in her heart every woman longs to be a man, bewailing her misfortune in being born a woman, and praying all her life for one thing only, to be born a man in another birth. And one thing above all she cannot understand, how or why any man should make a fuss about any woman, as all men do: which, just because she is not a man herself, she cannot comprehend. And like jugglers, that are not taken in by their own tricks, women look upon men as mere fools, for being taken in at all. For a woman's charm, to a woman, is not only not a charm at all, but a trick, and a lure, understood, and utterly despised. So now, be a man, and whatever folly thou art meditating, at least beware of being guilty of the very greatest of them all, by doubting of thy own superiority of manhood to the womanhood of any woman, no matter who she be: and earning her contempt, by lying at her feet. And now, farewell! for I have business with Narasinha.

And at the name of Narasinha, I pricked up my ears. And I said, with feigned indifference: Who is Narasinha?

And Haridása spat upon the ground. And he said: One, whom thou art lucky not to know: and yet, his name is *apropos*. For he is the Queen's lover, and an instance in point: since he leads her by a string, just because he treats her as a trifle, and not, as all her other lovers do, as a gem not to be matched by any other in the sea. And yet he is not, like thee, a man among men, but a man among women. For just as a dancing-girl loves to be treated as a queen, so does a queen love to be treated as a dancing-girl.

And then, all at once, he struck me on the shoulder. And he said, in a low voice: Why didst thou start, when I named Narasinha?

And without waiting for any answer, he got quickly on his camel, and rode away, never looking back.

XIII

And I stood, looking after him, with a startled heart, and then I went home slowly, saying to myself: How in the world did he guess my secret, and what did he mean? Was there a warning in his words? And what is all this about the Queen? Did he ever see her in his life? for if he had, he would long ago have discovered that all his rules have exceptions, of which Táráwalí is one: being not only the very gem beyond comparison that he spoke of with contempt, but a woman of women who very certainly never would despise any one at all, least of all the man who thought her exactly what she is, a star, far, far above his own muddy earth: a thing made of some rare celestial matter, differing altogether from anything to be found here below, fetched by the Creator when he meant to make her from some abysmal intermundane mine, where ocean foam and lunar ooze and sandal-wood and camphor lie jumbled up together with the essence of all curves and smiles and whispers and soft kisses and sweet glances and irresolution and long hair. And the image of the Queen rose up before me, laughing as it were in scorn at Haridása, and utterly obliterating everything he said. And I said to myself in ecstasy: Sunset will be here, very soon. And I reached my house, and looked, and lo! there was sitting at the door a Rajpoot, covered with the desert's dust, and holding by the rein a horse that hung its head, trembling still, and white with foam.

And as I came towards him, he stood up, and made obeisance. And he said: Maháráj, thou art come at last, and it was time. And I said: What is the matter? Then he said: Thy mother sent me, and I have ridden night and day. The King thy father is dying, and every moment he may be dead. And now, if thou carest, either for thy father, or thy mother, or thy throne, there is only one chance for thee, to fly to them as fast as any horse can take thee, without the delay of a single moment. So my message is delivered, and the Maháráj is judge.

And again he made obeisance, and went away on foot, leading his horse behind. And I stood, looking after him in a stupor, like one struck by a bolt from heaven, in the form of his appalling news. And I said to myself: Go I must, or my mother is ousted, and the *ráj* lost. And yet if I go, the sun will set in the Queen's garden, and I shall not be there.

And I pushed my door wide open, and went in, and sat down, with my face buried in my hands. And my own words sang in my head, over and over again: Go I must, or the *ráj* is lost, and my mother ousted. And the sun will set in the Queen's garden, and I shall not be there.

And I heard a laugh beside me, and I looked up. Lo! there was Chaturiká, standing in the open door! And she looked at me with laughing eyes, and she said: Ha! as it seems, I am just in time to save thy life: for thou art apparently all but dead. And, beyond a doubt, the Queen is a cunning doctor, who understands her patient's case. For she sent me to thee, saying: Go to him, O Chaturiká, since without thee he will die: and help him, how thou canst, to live until the sun has set.

And I stood up, and seized my hair with both my hands. And I groaned aloud, and said: Alas! O Chaturiká, what is a man to do, when two suns set, in opposite directions? And instantly, all the laughter died out of her face. And she looked at me with dark eyes, and she said: Two suns! What dost thou mean? And I told her all, and she listened in silence, till I ended. And then she said, with a sigh of relief: Ah! is that all? And I exclaimed: All? is it not enough for thee? And she said: I was terrified, by thy talking of two suns. For I began to think the Queen had a rival in thy affection. And I laughed, in anger and derision, and I exclaimed: A rival! Thou little fool! I am sorely tempted to beat thee, for daring to think anything of the kind, even in a dream. What! a rival! to Táráwalí! Thou art stark mad. How could she possibly have a rival in the three worlds? But what am I to do? And she said: It is thy choice, not mine. Only when once a sun has set, who can tell, if it will ever rise again? And what am I to say to the Queen?

And as she stood, looking at me, for an answer, there rose into my recollection the image of Táráwalí, leaning towards me in the moonlight, and saying: To-morrow, at sunset, I will be thy dream. And suddenly I exclaimed: Go back to her, O Chaturiká, and tell her that my only sun is the sun that sets in a Queen's garden.

And then, to my astonishment, that singular Chaturiká suddenly threw herself into my arms, and kissed me without waiting to be asked. And seeing me look at her in perplexity, she burst out laughing, and she said with delight: Ah! ah! So then, after all, there is a difference, as it seems, between Chaturiká and Táráwalí. No doubt some kisses are far sweeter, but the sun must set, ere the lovely digit of the moon rises, and I must do what I can meanwhile, to help thee to keep alive. It was her own order. And moreover she will not be jealous, and will not scold me when I tell her all about it on my return. And I said: Nay, thou saucy little beauty, tell her with all my heart, and add, that her drug was efficacious, since sandal-wood and camphor turn everything that touches them into a little bit of fragrance exactly like their own. And take her hand, and kiss it, and say I send the kiss, like her message, by thy mouth, and here it is.

And I caught her in my arms, and kissed her as she struggled, not willing this time to be kissed at all, exactly on her laughing lips, and then she went away.

XIV

And I said to myself in ecstasy, as she disappeared: Out on the very notion of leaving Táráwalí in the lurch, and losing the very essence of the nectar of the lady of my dream, so kind, so clever, and so wonderful as she is! Well did she understand, how the very sight of this audacious little *chetí* would act like a balm on the fever of my longing for herself: carrying about with her, as she does, a reminiscence of the intoxicating fragrance of the great champak flower, whose messenger she is, like a female bee, scattering another's honey as she goes. Aye! Chaturiká is like a letter, smelling of the sandal of the hand that wrote it, far away. And Táráwalí understood it all, and sent her; not being jealous, as Chaturiká says, and indeed, as she said herself, last night. As if a star of heaven could possibly be jealous of a little Ganges pot![27] Aye! little did my mother dream, when she sent to fetch me, what influence she had against her. As if I would purchase any kingdom in the world at the price of sacrificing my sunset with the Queen! And how can I help it, if the King my father chose just this unlucky astrological conjunction, to die? Or what good can be done by haste? For if he is dead already, as is very likely, all is lost, and it is useless to go at all. And if on the contrary, he lives for a little longer, I shall find him still alive, if I start to-morrow. And is it likely he will live or die exactly so, as to make my starting now either necessary or advantageous? And shall I take the risk, and throw away the very fruit of my birth, for nothing at all? And what would Táráwalí think of me, if I left her in the lurch, counting her inestimable favour as a straw? Beyond all doubt, she would wipe me from her memory as a thing beneath even contempt, like a sieve, all holes, into which it is futile to pour anything at all. No, I will keep my sunset, even if I lose my kingdom. And yet, why should I, after all? For to-morrow when I actually start, I will go very fast indeed, preparing everything beforehand, and having my horse waiting for me, so as to lose no time when I leave the Queen, carrying with me as I ride the memory of to-night: whereas if I threw her over, and set off to-night, the thought of what I was leaving behind would be so heavy as utterly to prevent me from going along at all.

And so I mused, waiting all the time with fierce impatience for the sun to sink, till at last day came to an end. And then I rose in delight, exclaiming: At last, at last, separation is over, and now it is time! And I went very quickly to the palace, and found the *pratihárí*: and she led me away straight to the door, and opened it, and I went in.

XV

And then, once more, I stood still, listening in ecstasy to the door as it shut behind me, and tasting, as it were, for an instant the delicious promise that the dusky garden gave me, standing like a diver on the edge of ocean, just before he plunges in, knowing well that it holds a pearl. And I stretched my arms towards the trees, saying to myself: This is not like the other times, but far, far better: for to-night she will not ask me to give her a music lesson, but she said herself, she would be my dream. And I wonder how she will do it, and what she is going to do. And then I went on through the trees, looking from side to side, with a soul as it were on tiptoe with curiosity and anticipation. And far away through the trees I saw the red rim of the full moon rising in a great hurry as if like myself he was dying with impatience just to see her, and saying as it were: I am the only lamp fit to light her, and I am just coming in another moment, like herself. And I passed by her swing that hung drooping, as it were, sadly from its tree, because she was not there. And little by little, my heart began to crave for the sight of her, growing restless and uneasy, and saying to itself with anxiety: What if something had actually prevented her from coming, and the garden were really as empty as it seems, and she were not here at all. And then at last I reached the terrace by the pool, exactly where I saw her first, and looked round with eager eyes, and she was not there. And then, just as I was on the verge of sinking into the black abyss of disappointment, all at once she came out of the shadow of a clump of great bamboos, in which she had been hiding, as it seemed, just to tease me into the belief she was not there, in order to intensify the unutterable delight of her abrupt appearance. And she stood still, as if to let me look at her, between two bamboo stems, just touching them with the very tips of the fingers of each hand, and saying in her soft sweet voice with a smile: Was I not right in choosing this as the only proper place for thee to meet the lady of thy dream, where we met each other first?

And I stood, confounded and as it were, dazed, by a vision so marvellously lovely that it puzzled me, murmuring to myself: Can this be Táráwalí after all, and what has she done to herself, for she has changed, somehow or other, into the incarnation of some deity exactly like her, and she looks like an image of the wife of Wishnu[28] that has somehow or other come down from its pedestal on a temple wall? For she was clothed in some strange colour that hovered between pallid yellow and deep red, seeming to have been borrowed from the setting sun and the rising moon. And it was all pulled forward, so that it clung somehow or other tight to her rounded limbs, making her whole outline from head to foot look like soft marble in the moonlit dusk, and it was collected in front into one great heavy fold that hung straight down like a red pillar from the very middle of her small waist, ending just above her feet in great gold tassels, that nearly touched the huge anklets of green jade with which her two little bare feet were loaded, as if to help them to stand firm. And a soft broad band of gold ran right round her just below her lovely breast, that lay held in its gold cup like a great double billow made of the creamy lather of the sea, prevented from escaping as it swelled up by the delicious dam formed by the curve of her shoulders meeting the soft bulge of the upper part of her rounded arms, which came out from each side and seemed as it were to wave gently in the air like creeper sprays, free and unconfined, and not like her feet, chained down, but absolutely bare of any ornament at all. And on her hair was not a star, but a great yellow moonstone, that shone with a dull glimmer like a rival moon of her own, and over her left shoulder a long coil of dark hair came out from behind her head and hung down like a serpent, ending in a soft wisp like a yak's tail that was tied round with yellow silk. And the only thing that she retained of what she was before was the intoxicating charm of the upright poise of her whole figure, which seemed to say to me as I saw it: I am the one thing about her which she cannot possibly hide or alter, let her do what she will.

And she stood quite still, as I gazed at her in ecstasy, lost in the wonder of my own eyes, looking back at me with her head just a little on one side, and her eyebrows just a very little raised, as if with appeal, and great soft sweet caressing smiling eyes. And then, after a while, she said, looking down: See, my feet are prisoners to-night, to do thee honour, as their lord, and they cannot walk fast or far, but it does not matter, as they will not be wanted, for I have a surprise coming for thee, by and by. But as to my arms, I thought it better to leave them without the encumbrance of any ornament at all. And she waved them gently in the air, and a little smile stole over her lips, and she said: It would only have been in the way, if the fancy should come upon thee to say good-bye in thy own fashion. And now, it was very difficult for me to know exactly what to do, so as to place the lady of thy dream before thee, since thou hast never told me what she looked like in the dream. And so thou must forgive me, if I have come in anything short of thy expectation, for I have done what I could. Art thou satisfied with her, as she stands? For if not, I must call my soul to the assistance of its body.

And I stood, unable to speak or move, gazing at her almost in a swoon by reason of the excess of my intoxication; and after a while, I drew a very deep sigh. And she came towards me, very slowly, as I stood rooted to the ground; and she put up her arms, and laid one hand on each shoulder, with a touch like the fall of a flake of snow. And she said: I know what is the matter: thou art spellbound by a return of thy original delusion. But it will leave thee, and thy senses will return to thee, once thou hast said good-bye. And then, seized with frenzy, I caught her in my arms, and suddenly she prevented me from kissing her by putting her hand over my mouth. And she said with a smile: Wait! Am I equal to Chaturiká, for as it seems, thou hast been playing me false? And for all answer, I took her hand, and kissed it, and put it round my neck, and then fell to kissing her in madness, continuing for I know not how long, bereft of my senses by the perfume of her hair and the touch of her arms. And then at last, I took her face in my hands. And I said: Away with Chaturiká! Thou knowest all, and art only jesting: and my soul quivers in my body at the sound of thy name. And she laughed, as I kissed her very gently on her two eyes, and she said: Perhaps I know: and yet, I will not forgive thee for Chaturiká, but on one condition. And I said: Ask anything thou wilt: it matters not. Then she said: Look at me very carefully, and think ere thou speakest: and tell me, exactly what it is, in me, that chains thee so to me, which Chaturiká and others are without.

And I said: Stand still, and let me look at thee, and think. And I put her away, and stood back, examining her very carefully just as she had wished, walking round and round her, and saying to myself: It is absolutely useless, for I know what to say without any need of looking, and yet I do not know if I can ever bring myself to stop, since she has given me, as if on purpose to delight me, a task more delicious than I ever had to do before. And all the time she stood absolutely still, patiently waiting till I ended, and looking at me every time I came round, with raised eyebrows and a smile. And at last, I could not endure it any longer, and I said: Ah! come back into my arms, which hunger for thee, and I will answer. And instantly, she came and stood, listening attentively, and caressing my ear unawares, as she listened, with her hand. And I said: Thy question is unanswerable, and my examination nothing to the purpose: since where was the use of looking at thy lovely body to find what is only to be found in thy soul, to which thy body owes the essence of even its own intoxication? For thy soul peeps out, from behind it, in the poise of thy head, and the straight erectness of its carriage, and the aroma of the royalty of sex that oozes, as it were, from its every gesture, mixed, in some unintelligible way, with a soft grace that seems to be all its own. But the spell thou art asking me to catch for thee looks from thy eyes, and lurks in thy lips, and murmurs in thy marvellous voice, which was silent all the while I was considering: and it is, some naive and submissive gentleness in the quality of thy soul, which turns all thy other perfections into instruments of delirium, and yet notwithstanding contradicts them all. For any other woman but thyself possessing even one of them would be proud, whereas thou dost not even seem to be aware that there is anything about thee other than the common. And as it seems to me, it is this, which is the core of thy irresistible fascination, giving to all thy particular elements of loveliness a kind of salt, that mixes with their sweetness to drive me mad.

And she looked at me silently with meditative eyes; and after a while she said slowly: I wish I were a man, only for a moment, to judge of myself and thy answer: for in one way thou art right, since I cannot understand why all men seem to lose their reason, as soon as they see me. And I said: There it is again, the very thing I spoke of, in thy words: and it is so simple, and yet so indescribably delicious, that very glad indeed I am that thou art not a man, but a woman, and that it is I that am the man. And it would be a crime in the Creator to gratify thy wish by making thee a man, who art the very essence of all womanly perfection and attraction. And for satisfaction of thy wish, look at thyself through my eyes, and thy wish is attained, since I am myself the very mirror provided thee by the Creator for that very purpose. And so learn, by my mouth, that thy spell is something in thee that resembles the peace of a forest pool. And even to-night, all the while we have been together, thou hast been, and art, so curiously quiet, like the breast of a swan, bathing in the water of passion and emotion without even getting wet, and like the snow of Kailàs, never melting even in the sun of noon.

And again she looked at me with curiosity: and she sighed, as if to dismiss what she could not comprehend. And she said: See! the moon has climbed high, and is gazing on the lotuses, and I am tired of standing, and the time has come to give thee thy surprise. And she drew me away by the hand along the terrace, and down its marble steps, till we came to a great tree that hung down over the water like an umbrella, leaning from the bank of the pool, so that nothing could be seen through its wall. And she took me and turned me with my face to the water, and she said: Stand here absolutely still, and do not look round, and I will bring thee thy surprise. And then she went quickly into the trees.

And I stood waiting, exactly as I was told, listening to her steps as she went away, and wondering where she was going, and what she was meditating, and what the surprise was, when it came. And so as I stood, I said to myself: Can I really be awake, or is it all only a long dream? For I seem to have been dreaming ever since I saw her first. And time slipped away, and still I stood, straining my ears for the sound of her steps returning, and dying to look round, but never looking, and haunted by a feeling that was almost terror, saying to myself: Why is she away so long, and what if she never returns at all?

And so as I stood, with my soul in my ears, turned as it were behind me, suddenly there came round the tree upon the water a great boat of the colour of a lotus leaf, turned up at each end like the neck of a swan. And it came straight towards me, and as it reached me, its boatman stood up, looking at me with a smile.

And I started, and all at once I laughed aloud, for amazement and delight: and even so, I hardly knew her to be herself. For she had cast away all her deity, and turned herself into a *chetí*, resembling a fragrant essence of midnight without a moon, clothed with absolute simplicity in soft dead black, with her own dark hair for her only decoration, tied in a knot around her head like a cloud of misty intoxication, and floating about her shoulders in confusion. And she looked at me with questioning eyes that shone bright in the moon's rays, and said naively, with a smile that almost broke my heart in two: Now I am within a little of being equal to Chaturiká? Is the maid a substitute for the queen that has disappeared?

And as I gazed at her in rapture without giving any answer, she said again: See! now we will float for a little while among the moon-lotuses, before we say good-bye. And this is thy surprise. And it is a delight that I keep for myself alone, and very few indeed are privileged to share it: but to-night, I am the lady of thy dream, and I will not do my favours by halves: and so thou shalt be my partner. And this is my swan's nest, and my floating cradle, in which I do my dreaming: for I can dream dreams as well as thou. And now I am going to dream a little, and we will dream together. And come, for the lotuses are waiting for us.

And I got into the boat, and pushed it out upon the water, and she came to me of her own accord, and locked her arms around my neck. And we drifted to and fro, exactly as the boat chose, on the silent black mirror of the pool, never saying a single word, but kissing each other insatiably with lips that were never tired, lost in the bottomless abyss of the ecstasy of mutual union. And all the time she bathed me with the beauty of her eyes, that like the pool, drew the moonlight down into their dark depths, caressing me with soft hands that touched me like the fall of a leaf, and lips that smiled and trembled like the shadows of the lotuses in the still water's swirl. And the moon rose higher and higher, and the night crept unobserved away, for I was utterly unconscious of the passage of any time. And then at last as I lay, worn out and overcome by the excess of my own emotion, and lulled by the gentle drifting of the boat, and wrapt in the delirium of oblivion arising from the unimaginable reality of the lady of my dream, unawares I fell asleep.

XVI

And when I awoke, lo! the moon was standing on the very edge of the western sky, and dawn was glimmering in the east. And the Queen was gone! And I leaped out of the boat, which was fastened to the bank, and ran up into the garden, which was as dark and as empty of anything living as a tomb. And after looking for her a long time in vain, at last in despair I went away to the door, and knocked, and it was opened; and there stood, not the *pratihárí*, but Chaturiká. And I said: Chaturiká, what has become of the Queen? And she said, with emphasis: Forget the Queen, and remember thy father: it is time.

And I started, as if she had run a poisoned needle into my ears; for I had utterly forgotten all about him. And no sooner had I got out of the palace than I ran all the way home through the empty streets. And I found my horse waiting, and I sprang on him, just as I was, and I went out of

Kamalapura, making for the desert as if I were running a race with the god of death, to determine which of us should reach my father first. And yet as I rode, I was thinking all the time of one thing only, to return, quicker even than I went away, and listening to my heart that sang without ceasing Táráwalí, Táráwalí, as if keeping time to the rattle of the hoofs of the horse. And after a while, I began to say: If I am to return, it will have to be on another horse: for whatever else dies, or does not die, this horse will die, beyond a doubt, either at the end of his race, or it may be, even before.

And it happened as I said. For suddenly the horse fell, to rise no more, while yet there was far to go: leaving me alone in the desert, with the sun right over my head. And I exclaimed: Alas! out upon fate, and out upon my own folly, for now I have killed my horse, that I loved better than my own soul! Alas! my horse was like my good fortune.[29] And if I had only started in the night, he would have had an easy journey, going slower in the cool hours. And I have offered my horse a sacrifice, and it may be, my kingdom also, to my deity Táráwalí. And yet, what does it matter, after all? Is she not worth all the horses, and all the kingdoms in the world? Aye! I would give them all, for another sunset like last night, with the lady of my dream. But what is to be done now? There is absolutely no help for it, and I must finish my journey how I can, going slowly on my own feet.

And as I said, so I did: and so it came about, that faint and tired and overcome, by hunger and thirst and the long journey and the fierceness of the desert sun, I began to reach my own city only as he was going down. And as I slowly drew near it, making all the haste I could, suddenly there fell on my ear a sound, coming to me from the city, that smote it like a blow. And I stopped short, to listen; and all the hair on my body stood erect. And I said slowly to myself: I have lost the race, after all, for they are wailing in the city, and it can be for one thing only, that it is widowed of its King. Aye! I am too late. And I have killed my horse for nothing, since Death has arrived before me, after all, having annihilated my competition, by taking my horse upon the way. And I have reached my journey's end, just in time to hear the wailing, as if Death were jeering at me, saying as it were in irony: They must travel very fast who think to outstrip me.

And I went on to the palace, never stopping at the gate to ask what I already knew. And they ran to warn my mother, and she came out of the women's quarters, and stood looking at me grimly, covered as I was with dust and perspiration, and almost ready to fall down, for sheer fatigue. And then she said: Fool! thou art too late, and thy brother has the throne. And now thou art little better than an outcast, and hast lost thy father, and thy crown, and me.

And I looked at her, and I said: When did the King die? And she said: Sunset.

And I uttered a shout of laughter, and threw my hands into the air, and fell at her feet in a swoon.

XVII

And when I had recovered, in a day or two, I came, so to say, to terms with my loss and my condition: saying to myself: After all, my father had to die, whether I came to him in time, or not: and I could not have saved his life, by my coming, no matter when I came. And so, the only thing I lost, by coming late, is my *ráj*. But what do I care for any *ráj*, which, in comparison with Táráwalí, resembles a mere pinch of dust, thrown into the other scale? Away with the miserable *ráj*! as if another sunset with the Queen would not be cheaply purchased at the price of all the kingdoms in the world! And I passed my days of absence in doing absolutely nothing but thinking of Táráwalí, and waiting, with a soul almost unable to endure, till the moment of return. And I sent a secret messenger to Kamalapura, saying to him: Go to the palace gate, and ask the *pratihárí* for a *chetí* called Chaturiká. And when she comes, tell her by word of mouth, so that nobody may hear thee but herself: Greetings to the Queen from Shatrunjaya, who has lost his throne on her account, and does not care. And when the obsequies are over, he will return to Kamalapura, on the night before the moon is full.

And having sent him off, I waited, while the obsequies went slowly on, with a soul that almost parted from its body with impatience for an answer to my message that might help me to keep alive, saying to myself: She cannot send Chaturiká, as she did before, since it is too far off for anything but a letter or a message, which will have to do instead. But neither a letter nor a message ever came: though in the meanwhile, my messenger returned with empty hands. And I tortured him with questions, but all he had to say was that Chaturiká had listened, and bidden him to go away. And notwithstanding my bitter disappointment, I racked my brain to find excuses for them both, saying: I am a fool. How could I expect any reply, since after all I never put a question, and silence was the only answer to be given: and beyond all doubt, she is waiting till I come? And is it likely that she would trust a message to a man she did not know? She is keeping her answer to be sent in the form of a summons on the eve of the full moon, which was the only answer I was asking for. And yet, in spite of all that I could think of to cool the fever that burned in my heart, I chafed and pined, sick with anxiety and disappointment, and longing in vain for the thing that never came. And I said sadly to myself: Well, only too well, she knew, that the very shadow of a sign of any kind, from her, would have set my heart dancing like a peacock at the first symptom of the coming of the rain. Or can it be, after all, that she really did send an answer, which has somehow or other lost its way? Aye! no doubt, it must be so, for she is kind, and could not bear to think of the misery she knew I must be suffering every moment that I am not by her side.

And so, perforce, I waited, gnawing at my own heart, until at last the funeral ceremonies were over. And instantly, I took leave of my mother, and turned my back on my relations, and set off at a gallop for Kamalapura, with my heart singing for delight, like an arrow from a bow.

XVIII

And I reached it, exactly as I said, on the eve of the full moon. And I said to myself, with exultation: Ha! to-morrow night, it will be full, and red, and round, exactly as it was a month ago, and shining as it did before, upon the boat, and Tárávalí, and me. And at the thought, I laughed aloud, for sheer joy, and came to my own door, and went in. And lo! the very first thing that I saw, when I entered, was my lute, lying on the floor with a broken string, and looking at me, as it were, with reproach. For a ray of moonlight fell exactly on it as it lay, as though to say: See! the moonlight falls not alone on happy lovers, but on those that are deserted! And my heart smote me, as I looked at it, and I exclaimed: Alas! my old love, thou art indeed discarded for another; for I have not given thee a single thought, ever since I saw her first. Bitter indeed must be the sorrow of one that is cast, like thyself, aside! And then, I threw myself upon my bed, forgetting instantly my lute and every other thing in the delight of the anticipation of the coming day. And I slept all night, floating as it were on a dark wave of the ocean of sweet expectation, and smiling so to say in my sleep.

And when morning came, I arose, and went to and fro, singing aloud for joy, and saying to myself: Now the moment of reunion approaches, and the miserable fever of separation is nearing its end, for the sun has arisen and is rushing to his home in the western mountain, and his race, and my desolation, will finish exactly together. And now, Chaturiká is on her way, and will soon be here, looking like the dawn of my delight in a delicious feminine form. And she will look at me with her laughing eyes, and murmur, Sunset, exactly as before: and exactly as before, I shall kiss her, and send her back to the Queen. And so I waited eagerly, on the very tiptoe of expectation, with my eyes fixed upon the door. But day slowly travelled on, and yet she never came. And little by little, my delight slowly turned into perplexity, and anxiety, till at last, as hour succeeded hour, each longer than a *yuga*, my heart began to sink, lower and lower still, and I became actually sick with the agony of my disappointment. For the sun was indeed rushing down into the night, and yet she never came. And time after time, I went to the door, and opened it, and looked out, but no Chaturiká was there, and nothing was to be seen but the people in the street.

And when at last night actually fell, and found me still waiting, I could endure no longer, but I threw myself upon my bed, and lay in a stupor in the dark, abandoning all hope, and on the very verge of crying like a child. And I said to myself: Is she ill, or is she dead, or has she gone away, or what on earth can be the matter? Or can it be, after all, that my messenger played me false, and never went? For if she really got my message, long ago she would surely have sent Chaturiká to summon me, knowing that it was impossible for me to come of my own accord, and that I should be sitting waiting with my heart on fire for her summons to arrive. And so I lay, tossing all night long sleepless on my bed, and cursing the moon, which poured as if to mock me a silver flood of light upon the floor, seeming to say: Think what a night it must be in the garden! until in an agony of reminiscence and humiliation, I turned my back to it, and lay with my face to the wall. And when at last day returned, I arose and sat, in deep dejection, worn out, and at my wits' very end, never even daring to look towards the door, which remained obstinately shut. And all day long I sat still in a kind of dream, neither eating nor drinking, and hopelessly waiting still. And at last once more the sun went down, after a day that was longer than a year, leaving me lying in the dark.

And I know not how I got through the night, which I shudder even to remember; but when morning came, I was within a very little of being mad. And burning with fever, hot and cold by turns, for sheer impotence I got up and went out, and wandered up and down the streets, till at last for weariness I was obliged to return, though the thought of my deserted house was almost more horrible than death. And all at once, I looked up, and lo! there was Chaturiká herself, coming towards me in the street.

XIX

And at the sight of her, my heart leaped into my mouth, for she resembled the very last link that joined me to the Queen, in a feminine form. But at the very moment that I saw her, she saw me also; and she turned away, pretending not to see me, and went round the corner into another street. And instantly, I leaped after her like a deer, and caught her, almost running to escape me. And then, seeing that there was absolutely no help for it, she stopped, and stood looking at me with defiance, like an animal at bay.

And presently I said: Dost thou not know me, that thou runnest so fast to get away? And she said: I never saw thee: I was only in a hurry. And I said: Now, from bad, it is worse; thou art lying. And why, instead of running away, art thou not rather hastening to meet me? Hast thou no message for me from the Queen? And she said: No: none. And I exclaimed: What! none? Did not my message come to thee? And she said, reluctantly: It came. Then I said: Then the Queen must know that I am here. And why has she never sent? And Chaturiká said: Is it for me to give orders to the Queen? How can I know why she does not want thy presence? If she did, she would send. I am not the mistress, but only the maid: is Chaturiká the equal of Táráwalí?

And as she spoke, the tears rose into my eyes, for I remembered the words of Táráwalí, as she stood up in the boat. And I took her by the hand, and looked into her eyes. And I said slowly: Thou knowest only too well, for if thou art not her equal, thou art at least her familiar. And now, then, cheat me not: since the matter is to me one of life or death. Am I thy enemy, or art thou mine? Was it not only the other day that thou didst kiss me of thy own accord, as I have sat, these last two days, hoping against hope for thee to come and do again? And what have I done, to bring about such change? I liked thee better, far better, laughing: thou wert so joyous, and so pretty, and like the ecstasy in my own heart, in a woman's form. Aye! as I looked at thee, it made my heart echo, to hear thee laugh, since we were both of us devotees of one and the same deity, Táráwalí, thy Queen and mine. And now, something has come about, I know not how, to spoil it all.

And as I spoke, all unconsciously I gripped the hand that I held of hers in mine, and it may be, that my hand whispered to her own what my voice alone strove in vain to say. For as I gazed at her in anguish, with tears in my eyes, strange! all at once I saw her face change, and her lip quiver, and tears stealing, as if against her will, into her eyes too. And she tried to laugh, without succeeding: and all at once, she squeezed my hand that held her own, with force. And she said, in a voice that trembled as it spoke, half laughing and half weeping: Nectar when she turns towards thee: poison when she turns away. And suddenly she snatched her hand away from mine, and turned as if to go.

And I took her by the shoulder as she stood with her face averted, and I said: See, Chaturiká, my life is in thy hands. Come, do me this last favour, and I will never trouble thee any more. Wilt thou go straight to the Queen, and say I met thee in the street, and somehow or other, by hook or crook, contrive, that she shall send for me again, and very soon, for otherwise I cannot live much longer? Wilt thou? Wilt thou? And she hung her head, and said in a voice so low that I could hardly hear it: I will try. And I said: Go then, for I will delay thee no longer. And yet, listen! Come to me often, as thou art passing by, for the very sight of thee is life.

And without speaking, she rolled her head up in her veil, and went away very quickly. And I stood, looking after her as she went: saying to myself: There goes my last hope. And lucky for me it was that I caught her: for without her, I would by this have driven my own sword home into my heart.

XX

And I went home feeling like a man saved from the very mouth of death, saying to myself: Now then, happen what will! for at least I have secured the key of the door leading to Táráwalí, in the form of her maid. And now, it may be, I shall see her very soon. For beyond a doubt, there has been some blunder, or perhaps she was occupied with business of moment, that left her no leisure for affairs like mine. And all my fears may have been in vain. And at least, I can wait with hope, and not as I did before, in horrible despair, cut off from every means of communication. And I sat with a heart almost at peace, prepared to wait till the coming of Chaturiká on the following day. But it turned out contrary to my expectation. For I had been waiting for little more than a single hour, when there came a knock at the door. And when I opened, there stood Chaturiká again. And she said rapidly: The Queen will await thee in the garden to-night at sunset.

And I exclaimed, with a shout of joy: Ha! sunset! It is as I thought. Well I knew there was some mistake, and that she could not fail. And beyond a doubt, she had forgotten the time, remembering only when reminded by thee. Victory to thee, O Chaturiká! for to thee alone I owe the sunset, and now I will give thee for it almost anything thou canst ask. And Chaturiká said: Give me nothing. And she stood in silence, looking at me with strange eyes, in which, as it seemed, pity and curiosity seemed to be mingled with compunction and some element that I could not understand. And suddenly she came to me, and laid her hand upon my arm. And she whispered very quickly, as if she was half afraid of what she said: Do not go. And then, she turned and vanished from the room, as if to escape before I had time to ask for explanation.

And I said to myself, looking after her in wonder: What! do not go? So then, as it seems, there will be danger. But little does she know me, if she thinks that any danger would keep me from the Queen. And indeed, in the garden there is room for any number of assassins, if Narasinha or anybody else were jealous of my visiting Táráwalí. Danger! And I laughed in derision, that was mixed with intoxication, as if the very notion of danger from a rival added, somehow or other, to the sweetness of anticipation, by stamping me as a claimant to the affection of Táráwalí who was greatly to be feared. And all at once, light broke in, as it were, upon my soul. And I cried out in ecstasy: Danger! Ha! at last, all the mystery is solved. It was danger that prevented my Táráwalí from sending me any message or bidding me to come. And all the while she knew it, and she had to be very careful, fearing for my life. And suddenly, I struck my hands together, and I cried: Ha! what a fool I am! Why, she told me so herself, when I saw her for the second time, and yet I had forgotten it. And all this while, in the peevishness of my own oblivion and presumption, I have been blaming her, expecting things utterly unreasonable, and loading her extraordinary sweetness with miserable suspicions arising from my own imagination, and the blindness of my insatiable passion. Ah! Táráwalí, forgive me if I wronged thee! But I will make it up to thee to-night, and beg for thy divine forgiveness at thy feet. And all this hesitation was all the while only on my account: and yet, brute that I was! I never guessed it, till Chaturiká gave me, as it were, a hint, and put me upon the scent. And what else was her delay but an irrefutable proof of her affection, showing that she chose even to allow herself to be misinterpreted rather than let me run on her account into the danger that she knew.

And instantly, all the clouds of darkness and desolation rolled away in a body from my soul, leaving it bathing in the ruddy glow of sunset, and passion, and emotion, exactly as it was before. And I waited, plunged in the ecstasy of reminiscence and anticipation, till at last the sun began to sink. And then, once more I went, on feet dancing with agitation and delight, to the palace gates, and saw the *pratihárí* standing waiting as before. And as I entered, never doubting that she had instructions of my coming, she barred the way, saying: What is thy business? And I said: I have come by appointment to see the Queen. Then said the *pratihárí*: Thou must come another time, for the Queen is not here.

And I stopped short, as if she had suddenly run a dagger into my heart. And I said in a low voice: Not here? It cannot be. Thou art mistaken. And the *pratihárí* said: There is no mistake at all. She is gone. And I said: Gone? Where? When? And she said: She went within this hour, to visit her maternal uncle; for want, as I think, of something better to do. And when she will return, I cannot say.

And then, my heart stopped. And I stood for a single instant, erect, and I turned, as if to go away. And all at once, there came from the very middle of my heart, a cry, that tore me as it were to pieces, and I fell in the street like a dead man.

XXI

And when I came back to myself, I looked, and saw an old man with a long white beard gazing at me with anxiety, sitting by my bed in which I was lying, having been brought home I know not how as I lay in a swoon. And when he saw me look at him, he began to rub his hands together, with a little laugh. And he said: Ha! then, as it seems, after all, thy soul has returned at last: and it was time. For it had been away so long that I was beginning to doubt whether it had not said good-bye to thy body, for good and all. And now it has come back after all, by the favour of Ganapati, and the help of the Ayurweda, and one of Dhanwantari's[30] most unworthy devotees. And I said slowly: How long have I been dead? Then said that old physician: It is now nearly sunset again, and thou hast lain there without moving ever since they brought thee here from the street, about the time of sunset, yesterday. And now what is it, that has struck thee down, as if by a thunderbolt? For how can the physician cure, unless the patient tells him of his case?

And I closed my eyes for a while, as if to rest: and after a while I said: O father, there is nothing to tell, to one of thy experience and skill: for since childhood, it happens to me, every now and then, to fall down and lie in a trance: and when once I come back, all is over, and I go on as before, till next time. And now there is nothing to be done, but for me to reward thee for thy care, to which I owe my life. And though it is a thing of little or no worth, I will count it, for thy sake, as if it were a thing of price. And I gave that old man gold, and sent him away delighted, for all I wanted was to be rid of him as quickly as I could, lest I should fall into a fever and begin to rave, and betray my secret against my will.

And then, for many days, I lay, living very slowly, like one in a long dream, drinking water, and eating almost nothing, and going over in my mind every detail of my life since first I saw the Queen. And it seemed to me, as I mused, as if I had died long ago; and everything appeared to me like something that had happened long ago, to some other than myself. And day very slowly followed day, and life came back to me as it were with hesitating steps, as though it knew that it was coming to one that scarcely cared to bid it welcome. And then at last there came a day when I looked about with curiosity to see what might be seen, and lo! there in a corner lay my lute upon the floor.

So, after a while, I said: Lute, canst thou tell me, how it feels to be discarded? And I went and took it up, and strung it, and began to play. And as fate would have it, there came over the strings as I touched them a sadness like my own, that seemed to say: Come, we are fellow-sufferers, and now let us weep together, since there is absolutely nothing else to do. And suddenly, the lute fell from my hands of its own accord, and I fell with it upon the floor. And I wept, as if my very soul was about to abandon my body, for sheer despair. And as I wept, I came slowly back to the self I was before; yet so, that the half of me was left behind, and lost for ever. And I said to myself: I have been robbed by Táráwalí of all that was worth anything in my soul, and it only remains to consider, what is the next thing to be done.

And that very evening, I went out of my house for the first time since I fell down. And avoiding the streets, I wandered along by bypaths, till I reached the river bank. And I hid myself in the bushes, and lay watching the sun go down across the river, and thinking of Táráwalí and her pool, till unawares I went to sleep. And how long I slept I know not, but I woke suddenly in the night, roused by the voices of two that were talking close beside me, not knowing there was anyone by, to overhear. And as I listened carelessly without curiosity, all at once there fell on my ear the name of Narasinha.

And instantly, I crawled, like a panther, little by little, nearer to those two talkers, until I could easily hear everything they said. And one was saying to the other: It will be very easy, and the reward is very large. Then the other said: But why does Narasinha want to have him slain at all? And the first voice answered: What a question! Anyone can see that thou art a stranger to this city. Dost thou not know that he is the lover of the Queen, aye! and so, that she is more than his life? And yet, for all that, he cannot keep her to himself, since she is not only a Queen, and above all his controlling, but also a lady of many lovers, roaming like a bee, from flower to flower, as she will, and yet leaving each in the lurch almost as soon as it is tasted, being as unsteady as the flame of a lamp in the wind, and as deep and as crooked as a river, amusing herself as if she were a female *trinamani*[31] by watching the irresistible effect of her own attraction on the straws that she finds and throws away, as soon as she has tested them, regardless of what afterwards becomes of them, since they are then absolutely useless, resembling mere husks, whose kernel she has eaten. And if he could bear to do without her, Narasinha would slay her out of jealousy with his own hands: but as it is, he cannot, however much she laughs in his face. And so he repays himself by wreaking his vengeance on her lovers, in lieu of herself: and one by one, they all pay the penalty of their presumption, in having anything to do with her, with their lives: giving him hard work to do, since she finds and casts off a new lover almost every day. And of all, the only one that has escaped is Shatrunjaya, the mad player, who lost his reason altogether when he found himself cast adrift without knowing why: and was accordingly passed over by Narasinha, as not even needing to be killed, since he was as good as dead already, and beyond the reach of revenge.

And the second voice said: What a fool must this Shatrunjaya have been, to go mad, over such an *abhisariká* as this Queen! Then said the first with emphasis: Thou art thyself the fool, speaking at random without ever having seen her: for she is a very Shrí, laughing all the other women to utter scorn; and small wonder that he fell a victim to such a spell, being as he is very young. And moreover, she is the cleverest woman in the three worlds, and easily persuades every lover that she is doing as he wishes to oblige him, and not as is really the case making him a puppet of her own. And not one of them all ever even knows of the existence of any other lover than himself. And Shatrunjaya is all the more to be excused, because she really took a momentary fancy to him, and cloyed him for a day or two with nectar that soon turned poison, as Chaturiká says.

And the second voice said: Who is Chaturiká? And the first replied: She is the niece of my cousin on the mother's side, and she tells me all. And Táráwalí took her for a confidential *chetí* on account of her cleverness and beauty: as well she might, since the little jade is very pretty, and clever enough to be prime minister to any king. And between the two of them, who are more than a match for any man that ever lived, Shatrunjaya had no chance at all. Little did he know Táráwalí, thinking to keep her beauty to himself, or confine the ocean of her charms to a tank! Poor fool! what a trick they played him! For Chaturiká says, that Táráwalí gave another lover the very *rendezvous* she fixed for him, bidding her *pratihárí* say she was gone. Well he might go mad, for as I think, any other man might lose his reason, to be kept standing outside the door, while his mistress was kissing another man!

And he laughed out loud, as he ended: but I rose up from the ground, drawing my *kattárí* from its sheath. And I leaped out of the bushes suddenly upon those two laughers, who took me for a ghost in the form of the god of death. And I struck at one with the knife, and as luck would have it, I all but severed his head from his body at a single sweep. And I turned upon the other as he stood terror-stricken, staring at me with open mouth, and I said: Thy jest was very good, but mine is better still. I am Shatrunjaya, and not mad after all: but thou shalt not tell my secret to Narasinha; whom I will send after thee in good time. And I struck the knife into his eye, so hard, that I could scarcely pull it out again by putting my foot upon his head.

And I left them lying, and went home quickly, laughing to myself, and saying: Now they are paid beforehand, with their work still to do, in coin very different from that of Narasinha. And his own turn will come, by and by. And I wonder whose life I have saved, for I never caught his name. But no matter: I have learned, what is left for me to do: and it only remains to determine on the way. Alas! Narasinha, thy star is beginning to decline. Thou hast just lost thy assassins, and presently I will deprive thee of Táráwalí, and last, I will rob thee of thy life.

XXII

And then, day by day, I rose early in the morning, and ate the breakfast of a bull-elephant, and went out into the streets, hunting, not for a forest beast, but for a human quarry. And I roamed up and down through the city all day long, examining everything I met that had the shape of a woman with the eye of a hunting leopard. And so I continued, day after day, without success. And then at last, on the night of the Dipáwali, when the streets were full of people, suddenly I saw her coming straight towards me. But she never saw me, by reason of the crowd: and the prey is not thinking of the hunter, when the hunter is thinking of the prey. And I hid myself in a doorway, and let her pass by; and I followed her with stealthy steps until at last she turned away into a narrow lane that resembled the jaws of death. And I caught her up with silent tread, and all at once I took her by the wrist as she went, with a grip like an iron band.

And she turned and saw me, and she started, and uttered a faint cry. And instantly I said: Cry out, even once, and I will sever thy head from its body. Make absolutely no noise, and I will do thee absolutely no harm. But come with me, for I need thee for a little while. I have been at pains to find thee, and now I will not let thee go. But unless thou dost exactly as I tell thee, I will treat thee as I did thy accomplice on the river bank, a little while ago. And she turned a little paler as she listened, understanding that I did not speak in jest. And I said: Go on before me, in silence, to my house, for well thou art acquainted with the way. And I will follow, just behind, and if thou makest, as thou goest, so much as a sign, thy head will roll from its shoulders on the instant. And she bowed her head, and went. And when we reached the door, I opened it and we went in. And I shut the door, and there was no other light than the moonlight, which fell in a flood upon the floor. And I said: Sit there in the moonlight, for I have something to say to thee. And she sat upon the floor, watching me with fascination like a bird before a snake.

And I walked to and fro before her, and suddenly I stopped, and I said: Tell me, O Chaturiká, what would the Queen say, if I told her of thy habit of babbling to thy relations of her secrets? And for answer, Chaturiká began to sob, grovelling upon the floor at my feet. And I said: Sit still, thou little fool, and listen: for thou shalt earn my forgiveness by doing as I bid thee: and if not, I will save the Queen trouble by becoming thy executioner myself. To-morrow night, I must see her in the garden as before: and it can only be by thy contrivance. And now, how is it to be done?

And Chaturiká said, weeping: To-morrow night it cannot be, since she has given that evening to another. And moreover, for thee every night is equally impossible, for she will not see thee any more. And how canst thou pass the *pratihárí*, or enter by the door, without her permission? And now between the Queen and thee, I am in the jaws of death. For thou wilt slay me, if I do not find thee entrance into the garden: and she will, if I do.

And I looked at her with scrutiny and I said: I will help thee out of jeopardy. There must be another entrance to the garden. Is there no other door? And she said unwillingly: There is, but none can enter from without, unless he has the key, which the Queen trusts to no custody but her own.

And I said: Then the way is found, luckily for thee: and thou art saved, since none will ever guess thy part in the arranging for my entry, if as I imagine thou art only sufficiently adroit to procure for me a key without her knowledge. And that I leave to thee, only be careful to bring it in good time, before to-morrow evening. And in the meanwhile, go and tell that other lover that the Queen has changed her mind: and put him off to any other day, it does not matter which, seeing that it will never come at all: since for the future, I am going to be the only lover of the Queen.

And then, Chaturiká looked at me in such amazement that it deprived her for an instant of her terror, and suddenly she began to laugh. And I stooped and lifted her, and whirled her in the air, and stood her breathless on her feet. And I took her two hands and held them tight, and I said: Dost thou feel what thou art in hands like mine, a feather, and a nothing, and a straw? Now listen and be wise. Stand out of the way, between the Queen and me, for we shall crush thee, and the battle is one that I mean to win. And now I am going to show her something that she never saw before, the strength of a man: for a woman presumes, forgetting altogether that she owes all to the forbearance of one who can sweep her away if he chooses, like a wild elephant snapping a twig. And if anything goes amiss by any treachery of thine, I will break thee in pieces with my bare hands, hide where thou wilt, making it unnecessary even to betray thee to the Queen. And now, what have I ordered thee to do?

And Chaturiká said humbly, quivering like a wild heifer that is suddenly tamed by the sound of a tiger's roar: To put off a lover and bring thee a key.

And I said: Thou hast still forgotten the thing without which both are useless, and that is, to show me the outside of the door to be opened by the key. And that thou shalt do at once. Go out now, and walk without stopping straight to the door: and I will follow in thy steps. And do not look back, until thou art standing just beside it, and then turn for a single instant, and meet my eye without a sign. And then begone where thou wilt until to-morrow.

And I opened the door and let her out, and she went away very quickly, leading me through the city and past the palace gates, and a long way round the palace wall, until at last she suddenly came to a dead stop, beside a little door in the wall, that stood exactly opposite a ruined temple of the great god. And there she turned and looked at me, and then continued on her way until she disappeared. And I stood and watched her go, saying to myself: I think she will bring me the key to-morrow, without dreaming of betraying me: for I scared her almost to death, and she is frightened. And I was very sorry for her, and yet it was the only thing to do, for there was no other means of reducing her to absolute submission. And yet she was beautiful to look at, even so, resembling as she did a feminine incarnation of audacity suddenly changed into unconditional obedience by standing between two appalling dangers, and only doubting which was the most to be feared. And very strange is the difference fixed by the Creator between a woman and a man: since the very timidity that makes him utterly contemptible only makes her even more beautifully delicious than she was before.

XXIII

And next day, I waited all the morning for Chaturiká to come, and noon arrived without her coming. And I said to myself as I sat waiting: She will come by and by, and I cannot expect her very early, for she may have many other things to do as well as mine. And it may be no easy task that I have given her to do. And now, what am I to say to Tárávalí, when I come upon her in the garden, and see her, O ecstasy! again? And strange! at the very thought of seeing her again, my heart began to burn, as if turning traitor to my own determination. And I said sadly to myself: Alas! I am afraid, or rather I am sure, that the very sight of her will be like a flood, in which every fragment of my resentment against her for treating me as she has done, and every atom of my resolution, and every recollection of all that I have heard to her discredit, will be swept away like chips and straws. Do what she may, I cannot drive my affection for her out of my heart, which obstinately clings to her image, utterly refusing to be torn away. And notwithstanding all that those two rascals said in her disparagement, my soul laughs them to utter scorn, telling them they lie. And who knows? For who could believe that a body so unutterably lovely could harbour a soul so unutterably base as they said, on evidence such as theirs? Aye! my recollection of her soul is an argument in her favour that nothing that they said can overcome, and I could forgive her absolutely anything, when I think of the gentle sweetness that echoed in her every word, resembling a perfume somehow mixed with her voice. And yet if my resolution wavers, even now, how will it be when she actually stands before me as she will to-night? And yet, how is it possible to absolve her for her inexplicable behaviour to me?

And so as I mused, touching all unconsciously the strings of my lute which was lying in my hands suddenly a thought came into my mind of its own accord. And I took the lute and unstrung it, and chose from among its strings one, which I rolled like a bangle on my wrist. And I said to the lute aloud: Old love, we will work together: for if indeed she is my enemy, she is thine as well. And if, as those assassins said, she is only a body without a soul, playing on us both merely for her own amusement, then we will give her together a music lesson of a novel kind, and teach her that the deadliest of all poisons is a love that has been betrayed.

And suddenly I heard loud laughter, like an echo to my words. And I looked up, and lo! there was Haridása, standing in the open door. And he said: What is this, O Shatrunjaya? Whom art thou about to poison, or who is going to poison thee? And hast thou solved thy problem, since I saw thee from the camel's back, pondering on thy own beauty? Or hast thou arrived already at the poison in the bottom of love's cup? How is good advice thrown away upon a fool! Did I not warn thee? Wilt thou never understand that the nectar of a woman is like the red of dusk, lasting for but an instant, and like the cream of milk, turning sour if it is kept, and like foam of the sea, which exists only during agitation, melting away into bitterness and ordinary water as soon as it is still? As indeed every woman well knows, without needing to be told, and therefore it is that she is nectar always to a stranger, and insipid, even when she is not very disagreeable, to her friends, losing her fascination, like the thirst of the antelope[32] on Marusthalí, for all that approach her too near: since all her delusion depends upon her distance, and vanishes altogether by proximity. Keep her always at a distance, O Shatrunjaya, if thou art anxious to remain under the spell.

And I said: Haridása, I am only a fool, as thou sayest, but thou art wise. And now, wilt thou serve me at a pinch, by something more than good advice? And he said: By what? Then I said: To-night, I have business that I cannot avoid, and yet I cannot go out, unless I can find one whom I can absolutely trust to remain here till morning in my place, to guard a deposit. And so, wilt thou be my guard? And Haridása said: I cannot refuse, if thy need be extreme. For men to be absolutely trusted are very rare, and I am one. And is thy deposit large? And I laughed, and I said: Nay, on the contrary, it is very small. And it will be here in another moment, for I have been waiting for it all day long. And as I spoke, lo! Chaturiká appeared in the door, as if by a toss of the curtain,[33] And I said to Haridása: Here it is.

And seeing that I was not alone, Chaturiká turned, as if to go away. And I called out to her, saying: Wait but for a single instant, O thou destitute of patience, and give me back my key that I gave thee last night, since I am in sore need of it. And then she came to me in silence and gave me a key. And I said: Hast thou put off the petitioner as I desired, to another day? And she said: Yes. And then I went to the door, and shut it. And I said to Haridása: I have an appointment, with one who may be friend or foe, for I cannot tell. But here is a hostage, that I leave behind me. Keep her for me, and never take thy eyes off her, and give her back to me, safe and sound, on my return. But if the sun rises to-morrow, and I am not here, cut her head off, for she will have led me into a trap, all unaware that she was setting it for herself as well.

And Haridása looked thoughtfully at Chaturiká as she stood aghast, rubbing his chin with his hand. And he said slowly: It would be a great pity, my pretty maiden, if he came late, for thy head looks very well as it is on thy little body, which without it would look as melancholy as a palm broken short off by the wind.[34] And yet, do not weep. For Shatrunjaya is a bad judge of men and women, and I am a very good one. And if, as I think, he is altogether wronging thee by his suspicion, thou hast absolutely nothing to fear from me, and I will be thy father and thy mother till he returns to free thee in the morning. So dry thy tears, and I will return to thee in a moment to make thee laugh.

And he led me away out at the door, and shut it behind him. And he said: Shall I tell thee the name of thy very pretty deposit? Dost thou think I do not know what thou art endeavouring so clumsily to hide? Nectar when she turns towards thee: poison when she turns away?

And as I started, staring at him in stupefaction, he said with a laugh: Ha! thou hast heard it before? Didst thou not betray to me thy secret unawares, repeating it before? What! dost thou not know, it is the Queen's verse, which all the people in the city sing of every man who dooms himself by becoming the Queen's lover? I could have told thee, even without seeing Chaturiká at all, that it was Táráwalí herself who was thy nectar, and is going to be thy poison; and well I understand who is the friend or foe to whom thou art just about to go. It is the Queen.

And he took me by both hands, and looked straight into my eyes. And he said: Fool! and art thou actually hoping still for the nectar that is gone? Thy hope will be in vain. I told thee, without naming her, to hold her very cheap, if ever thou wouldst have her hold thee dear. It was useless to restrain thee, for thou wouldst not have believed me, no matter what I said. There was but a single chance. For the moment that she sees that her fascination works, and that her lover lies gazing without reason or senses at her terrible beauty, she is satisfied, and throws him away: whereas had he only the strength to resist it, she might against her will fall in love with him herself for sheer exasperation at her impotence, in his case alone. But she swept thee clean away like a straw in a flood, and thou art lost. Thou hast been playing unaware with a queen-cobra, that has smitten thy soul with the poisonous fascination of its magnificent hood and its deadly eyes, and bitten thy heart with its venomed fang; and now all remedies are worse than useless, and come too late. I can see death written on thy brow, and almost smell its odour in the air. Beware of Narasinha!

And he went in, and shut the door upon himself and Chaturiká, leaving me alone in the street.

XXIV

And I stood in the street, staring at the door as it shut behind him, as motionless as a tree. And I murmured to myself: Nectar when she turns towards thee: poison when she turns away! So then, it is the Queen's verse, sung of others and sung of me! And this was the meaning all the time! And this is what Chaturiká was thinking of, every time she said it, laughing at me in her sleeve, as beyond a doubt she has laughed at many another man before! And this is what the people say! And all the time I thought myself exceptional, I was only being made a fool, and one of a large number, and a laughing-stock for the whole city, and branded, as it were, with ridicule and ignominy as a plaything of the Queen, and going about unconsciously with her label round my neck: Nectar when she turns towards thee: poison when she turns away!

And suddenly, rage rushed into my heart in such a flood that it felt as if it were about to burst. And from motionless that I was, I began all at once to run in the direction of the palace, as though about to wreak my vengeance on the Queen without waiting for a single instant. And then I stopped abruptly and began to laugh. And I exclaimed: Am I actually going mad, for as yet it is still day, and I cannot even get into the garden till the sun has set. And after thinking for a moment, I went away to the river bank to wait till the sun was down. And there I threw myself down at full length upon the ground, with my chin upon my hands.

And then, strange! as I lay, little by little my heart began to cool, and all its fury ebbed gradually away. For as I thought of Táráwalí, it seemed as it were to say to me: I cannot find room, on second thoughts, for any rage at all, since I belong absolutely to the Queen. And all my rage turned slowly into such unutterable longing that her image seemed to grow dim, seen through the mist of eyes that were suffused with tears, as recollection brought her back to me saying: This is how she looked when she saw thee first, and this again, is how she lay in the swing, and this again, when she stood up before thee, as a *chetí*, in the moonlit boat. And I exclaimed in desperation: Alas! O Táráwalí, must I then condemn thee, whether I will or no? For they all say the same of thee, and as it might seem, it must be true, and yet no matter, for I absolutely cannot either hate thee or believe them, when I think of thee as I saw thee myself. And my heart laughs in scorn at all the efforts of my reason, never wavering for an instant from thy side, like an incorruptible ally, that cannot be induced by any bribe whatever to abandon its allegiance. Aye! would she but open her arms to me again, I should forget everything else in the three worlds, to snatch her in my own. How is it possible to hate her? And beyond all doubt, that rascal I slew hit the mark, when he said that Narasinha cannot quarrel with her, being utterly unable to do without her, disarmed in all his attempts to oppose her by his own conviction that she is absolutely indispensable to his own life. For she may have deserved ten thousand deaths, and yet what does it matter, if for all that she is a thing that once lost or destroyed can never be replaced, as indeed she is, resembling the *Kaustubha*,[35] or the third eye of the Moony-crested god, of which in the three worlds there is only one. And so since he cannot do without her, she is beyond all reach, and invulnerable, doing with impunity exactly what she pleases, caring nothing whether he loves or hates her, and laughing at the very notion of being brought to book, secure in the magic circle of her own irresistible attraction, whose very power of destroying all others is her own protection, like a spell with a double edge, such that, as that rascal said, she cannot refrain from amusing herself by trying its effect on all.

And who could find it in his heart to blame her for delighting in the exercise of her own spell, like a child rejoicing in its toy, aye! even were he himself its victim, as its effect would be the same, no matter what she did, seeing that she must attract whether she will or no? Being what she is, she cannot help it: it is involuntary and beyond her control. And alas! I fell before it without a shadow of resistance, enslaved even before I saw it by her own dream, not even affording her the pleasure of watching her fascination gradually overcoming opposition, and asserting its power, and subduing me to her domination, against my will. And so I became a thing of no value to her at all, since in my case there was nothing to overcome. Ah! had I only been capable of seeming to be one on whom her charm would not work, then indeed, as Haridása says, I might have prevailed: and she might herself have fallen victim to the man who defied her fascination and laughed in her face, out of pique and irritation at her own impotence. And all the more, if what that rascal said have any truth, that she actually took a momentary fancy to me, strange as it seems. But alas! as he said, it is all too late.

And suddenly I started to my feet with a beating heart. And I exclaimed: Too late! But what if it were not too late, after all?

And as I stood, thinking of it, struck into sudden agitation by my own idea, hope glimmered in the darkness of my soul like the first faint streak of rosy dawn at the end of a black night. And the dream of the bare possibility of bringing back Táráwalí with all her old intoxicating sweetness almost took away my breath. And after a while, I said to myself: Yes, indeed, he actually said, that she took a fancy to me, even though it were only for a moment. And how could he have known it, if she had not herself confessed it to Chaturiká, from whom alone he could have heard it, since very certainly he never learned it from Táráwalí herself? Aye! and was not Chaturiká herself far sweeter at the beginning, just as if she knew I was no ordinary lover, but one with a little foothold in the Queen's heart? And if, then, I was ever there, why could I not return? And if her fancy has gone to sleep, could I not awake it? Can it be already so absolutely dead as never to revive, with not a single spark among the ashes to be refanned into a flame? How would it be, could I but manage to persuade her she was utterly mistaken, in supposing that I was only a miserable victim of her spell? How, if I could convince her that I valued all her fascinations at a straw? Would she not at least be tempted to try them all on me again, if only to test them and discover whether I was lying or in very truth proof against all the power of her charm? And if only she did, what then? For once she began, it would all depend on me, whether she ever stopped any more.

And all at once, I uttered a shout of hope and exultation and excitement, suddenly taking fire at the picture painted by my own craving imagination. And I exclaimed: Ha! who knows? And at least, I can try. And even if I fail, it cannot possibly be worse than it is already, drowned as I am in misery without her: whereas, if I could succeed! Ah! I would barter even emancipation for a single kiss! And O that my courage may not fail, turning coward at the very first sight of her again! For the struggle to appear indifferent, in such an ocean of rapture, will be terrible indeed, since even now, the very thought of it makes me tremble, being enough to make me fall weeping at her feet. And now the sun is setting, and it is time to go: and in a very little while, fate will decide, whether she and I are to die or live. For I cannot live without her, and unless she will allow me to live with her, she shall not live at all, either alone, or with anybody else. For she will kill me, by driving me away, and I will take her with me, if I am to die.

XXV

And then I went away with rapid steps, all through the city, till I reached the little ruined temple, that stood exactly opposite the door that Chaturiká had shown me the night before. And I hid myself behind the image of the Moony-crested god, and watching my opportunity that none should see me, all at once I crossed the street and tried the key in the door, almost shaking with anxiety, lest after all she had played me false, by giving me at haphazard some key that would not fit. But O joy! the key turned, and the door opened, and I went through. And very carefully I closed it again, and then, first of all, I hid the key in a hole in the wall, making sure of my return. And then I drew a deep sigh, almost unable to believe myself once more in that garden which held Táráwalí hidden somewhere in its dark recesses. And I said to myself, with emotion: Ah! now, come what may, at least I shall look upon her again, and very soon. And even for that alone, I am ready to die. And it may very well be that death is close at hand. For if Chaturiká is in the pay of Narasinha, as she very well may be, and has betrayed me, I may be walking straight into a trap. For his assassins may be posted in the trees in almost any number. And little should I care to die, so long as they only slew me on my return; but I am terribly afraid of being slain before I see her. For then indeed I should suffer the agony of a double death.

And I went on slowly in the shadow of the trees, guessing my direction, for I was going by a way I did not know, fearing not at all the death that might suddenly spring out upon me, but dreading far more than death the possibility of its anticipating my discovery of the Queen. And little by little, as nothing happened, I forgot my fears, saying to myself: To-morrow I will give Chaturiká anything in the world, and beg her pardon for suspecting her of breaking faith. But in the meantime, I must above all manage to come upon Táráwalí unawares, and escape her observation until I catch sight of her myself: for if she saw me first, she might hide, or even go away altogether, leaving me to look for her in vain, and making all assassination superfluous, since if I do not find her I shall simply die of my own accord, long before morning, of disappointment and despair. And so I went on very slowly, making absolutely no noise, like a Shabara stalking a wild elephant in the forest, dying of expectation, and yet not daring to make haste, for fear of losing all: until at last, after a very long time, I came to the terrace by the pool once more. And then I looked, and suddenly I caught sight of her, standing alone, like a pillar, on the very verge of the terrace steps.

And I stopped short in the shadow of a tree, to watch her for a little and master my emotion, holding my breath, and lost, not only in the ecstasy of being close to her again, but in sheer admiration of the wonder that I saw. For she was dressed as it seemed all in silver gauze, looking ashy pale in the moonlight, and she was standing absolutely straight up, with her two hands clasped behind her head, turning half towards me, so that I could just see her dark hair between her two bent arms, lit up not by a star, but a diadem like a young moon, that shone all yellow as if made by a row of topaz suns, so that she looked like a feminine incarnation of the Moony-crested god, smeared with silver sheen instead of ashes. And as she stood still with her two feet close together, gazing at the pool, with her head leaning a little back against the pillow of her hands, alone in the very middle of the terrace on the very edge of its top step, with nothing but the dusk for her background, resembling a great jar, her solitary silent figure, rising from its narrow base into lustrous moonlit curves that ended in the tall bosses of her breast, spread wide by her opened arms, stood out in a vision of exact and perfect balance, so marvellously lovely, that as I gazed at it, remembering how I held it in my arms, unable to contain my agitation, I uttered a deep sigh.

And instantly, she spoiled the picture, by changing her position, and looking straight towards me. And not being able to see me clearly by reason of the deep shadow that obscured me, she came back along the terrace in my direction, walking exactly as she did before, with the same intoxicating straightness of carriage, and the same rapid and undulating step, till I could have laughed aloud for very joy to see her coming to me, like the desire of my own heart incarnate in her round and graceful form. And as she reached me, she said, with exactly the same low and sweet and gentle voice that I was yearning with all my soul to hear again: Thou art late, for I have been waiting for thee a long time.

And suddenly I came as it were to myself, on the very verge of ruining all, by falling at her feet:[36] saying to myself with an effort: Now then, all is lost beyond redemption, unless I play the man. And I came out of the shadow, saying with obeisance: O lovely Queen, that is thy own fault, and not mine.

And she started back, with a faint cry, exclaiming in the extremity of sheer amazement: Shatrunjaya! How in the world hast thou got in here?

And I answered with a smile, though my heart beat like a drum within me: Ah! thou delicious Queen, in this lower world many things come about contrary to expectation, of which this is one. And if thy own surprise is extreme, so is mine: since, as it seems, my coming is not only unexpected, but unwelcome. And yet how short a time it is, since thou didst entertain me with a sweetness so extraordinary, and so spontaneous, and so mutually tasted, that I thought only to give thee pleasure by repeating the experience, and that is why I came. And if thou art sorry to look at me again, I do not share in thy feeling, since all the pains I have taken to arrive are repaid by even a single glance at thyself. For surely even Indra's heaven cannot hold anything so unimaginably lovely as thou art to-night.

And still she stood, gazing at me with strange eyes, and she murmured to herself, half aloud: Shatrunjaya! It cannot be! And I said: Nay, thou very lovely lady, but it can: since here I am, and I am I. And why not? Didst thou think I had forgot, what could not easily be forgotten, how we floated together in thy cradle among the lotuses? Or is it any wonder if I have thought of nothing else, ever since, but how to return? But as to how I came, it is a secret, that I do not choose to tell, since the fancy may take me to come again. And judging by thy excessive condescension when we met before, I did not think very much to displease thee, if I ventured to substitute myself this evening for another, who cannot even hope to rival me in the only thing that matters, my unutterable adoration of thyself: since of thy favour we are both of us equally unworthy. And yet, if, as it seems, I was utterly mistaken and the substitution is not to thy taste, I can very easily atone for my blunder by going away again at once. Dost thou really imagine me one to force himself upon a lady who wishes him away? O thou very lovely Queen, not at all. For I am just as good a man among men, as thou art a woman among women: and if I am not to thy taste, then, O thou fastidious beauty, neither art thou to mine. For the essence of every lovely woman's charm is her caress, which springs from her affection, and the desire to make herself nectar to her lover, without which salt, even beauty is beautiful in vain. And I care absolutely nothing for a beauty that does not take the trouble to be sweet. And well I know, by experience, how sweet thou canst be, aye! sweeter by far than any honey whatsoever, if it pleases thee to try. So choose for thyself, whether I shall stay, and revel like a great black bee in thy sweetness, as once I did before; or go away. But let me tell thee, pending thy decision, that if thou dost not take thy opportunity when it offers, it will never more return; for as I said, I do not like coming where my coming is met with distaste. But as I think, if thou wilt allow me to advise thee, and help thee to decision, we may as well make the most of one another, now that we are here, otherwise the moonlight will be wasted altogether, since to-night at least, thy other lover will not come. For I have taken care to exclude him, and we shall not be disturbed by any disagreeable interruption. And so, either thou wilt have to do without a lover altogether, or take me, for sheer want of something else. And the first would be a pity, and all the delicious trouble thou hast taken to deck thy beauty for its proper object, the delight of a lover, would be lost. For in thy silver ashes and thy moony tire, thou needest no third eye to destroy thy enemies, since thy divinity is so overpowering that not to employ it as it was designed to be employed would be a crime.

XXVI

And all the while I spoke, she stood, as curiously still as if she were made of marble, looking at me quietly, with her head thrown just a little back, and her left hand pressed very tight against her breast, and eyes that I could not understand. For they rested on me absolutely without anger, seeming as it were not to see me at all, but filled with some strange perplexity, as if she were hunting for something in her recollection that she could not find. And when I ended, she continued to stand, exactly in the same position, for so long, that I began to wonder what could possibly be passing in her soul. And I said to myself, as I waited in terrible suspense: Now very likely, in another moment, she will summon her attendants, and have me ejected, as well she might, for my almost inconceivable impertinence, which almost broke my own heart in two, to utter it at all. And if so it seems, even to myself, what must it seem to her? Aye indeed! for every word, I deserve ten thousand deaths, and I could forgive her, no matter what she did. Aye! and if, in a very little while, she does not speak, I shall be throwing myself at her feet and begging to be forgiven, unable any longer to endure.

And then at last, all at once, her tension relaxed, and she sank back suddenly into her old soft sweetness, with a deep sigh. And her eyes seemed, as it were, to come back to me, and find me for the first time, and there stole over her lips a little smile. And as I saw it, my heart almost broke with delight, for I said to myself: She has changed her mind about me; after all, and now my plan is beginning to succeed. Alas! little did I fathom the unfathomable intelligence of that extraordinary Queen! And presently she said, with exactly the same gentleness in her low voice that made my heart tremble exactly as before, every time it spoke: Thou art, beyond all doubt, the very first man in all the world, not only for effrontery and impertinence, but also, for this, that thou hast succeeded in imposing upon me, which no man ever yet did before. For in my simplicity I had thought thee quite another, making in thy solitary instance a mistake, unusual with me, and making me ashamed: since as a rule, men's hearts are no secret for my own, and I read them at a glance.

And she looked at me with a smile, and inscrutable clear eyes, whose expression was a puzzle to my soul. And I said: Then, since thou readest hearts so easily, why couldst thou not read mine also, as it is very plain thou didst not? And she said: Why very plain? And I said: Why didst thou send no answer to my message, and why didst thou summon me at sunset, and yet go away, leaving me nothing but the scorn of thy servants at thy gate?

And she looked at me in blank amazement, and she said: What dost thou mean? I never got any message, and if any summons came to thee, it was not sent by me. For I have not heard anything of thee at all, since I left thee at midnight in my boat.

And as she spoke, there came a mist before my eyes, and all the blood in my body rushed suddenly into my heart, as if to burst it, and then as suddenly left it, so that I almost swooned. And all at once, I exclaimed with a shout: Chaturiká! Ah! then I was deceived! Ah! then it was not thou! Ah! then I was not slighted by thee as a thing to be despised! Ah! then thou art not as they say, one that forgets and throws away her lovers almost as soon as she has seen them first! Ah! had I only known, I never would have stolen unawares into thy privacy to-night! Say, say, that thou art not such a woman as they say!

And again she looked at me, with those strange quiet eyes; and after a while, she said with a sigh: Thou art right. They say, but they do not understand. And yet, what does it matter what they say? Is it my fault, if every man that sees me is seized as it were with madness, and instantly steps over the line that divides friendship from passionate affection, asking me for what I cannot give him, with such eager insistence, that in my own defence I am driven to dismiss him altogether? And she smiled, and she said, with playfulness and wistful eyes: Must I belong to everyone, merely because he claims me as his own, and his property, and give myself to everyone that sees me in a dream?

And I trembled from head to foot, and I said in a voice that shook with entreaty and emotion like a leaf: Ah! then have I thy permission to stay with thee to-night, notwithstanding my overweening presumption in coming of my own accord without an invitation? Ah! I did not know: my heart is breaking: do not send me away!

And as she stood, looking at me with irresolution, I stretched my hands towards her, absolutely senseless, and not knowing what I did. And she hesitated for yet a little while; and then, with a sigh, she put her two hands into my own. And with a shudder of joy, I pulled her to me, and caught her once more in my arms, and began to kiss her, with hot tears that fell upon her face, quivering all over with the extremity of my agitation, and not believing that it was not a dream.

And then, after a long while, I came, somehow or other, to my senses, and became, a little, master of myself. And I looked at her with eyes dim with affection, and I took her two arms, and put them round my neck. And I whispered in her ear: Now give me a kiss for every day that I have not seen thee, since I fell asleep in thy boat. And as if with resignation and compliance and submission to my will, she did exactly as I told her, stopping time after time, but I would not let her stop. And at last, I stopped. And I said: There are more still owing, for thou hast not counted right. But now I will ask thee a question, just to give thee time to breathe.

XXVII

And as I held her still in my arms, with her own arms round my neck, she said: Ask. Then I said: Didst thou know, when I came to thee last time, that my coming delayed me in a matter of life and death? And she said: Something I knew, from the chatter of Chaturiká. And I said: Didst thou know that my kingdom depended on my going fast? For as it is, I lost it, all by coming late. And she said: It was no business of mine. And I said: What! wouldst thou deprive me of a kingdom, by placing thyself, for a single sunset, in the other scale? And she said: I did not bid thee stay. I had sent to thee already, asking thee to come: and if another summons called thee, after mine, the choice was thine, between them. I told thee only, I awaited thee: and it was true. And I said: What if I had not come? And she said: Then it may be, thou wouldst have kept thy kingdom, and lost thy interview with me. That is all. It was not I, who had anything to do either with causing thy dilemma, or determining its conclusion. And I said: Beyond a doubt, the loss of any kingdom would be a trifle in comparison with thy affection: and yet the loss is certain, and the affection doubtful. For I showed thee very plainly which I chose, and my kingdom is gone. I have thrown it clean away for thy sake. And have I its equivalent? Wilt thou make it up to me by giving me thy soul? And she said, gently: It is not mine, to give away, for I belong to Narasinha, body and soul, as I told thee long ago.

And I said: How canst thou say so, when I hold thee in my arms? And she said, quietly: Thou art but a momentary accident, due rather to my yielding myself, against my own will, and of pity for thy unhappy passion, than to any hold that thou hast on my heart. And Narasinha learned of thy former visit to me in this garden, as very soon he will learn of this also, since I tell him every detail of my life, great or small. And he made me promise never to see thee any more. And so I had intended: but thou hast managed to steal in, somehow or other, of thy own accord. It is not by my doing that thou art here now at all.

And I let her go, and stood gazing at her with amazement, that was mixed with bitter disappointment and irritation, and fierce exasperation at this obstacle of Narasinha, who, out of my reach, and hiding behind her as a screen, issued orders that I was to be shut out of her garden and banished from her presence, whether she would or not. And my heart swelled with resentment and indignation, and I said: O Táráwalí, Narasinha may shut his eyes, or not, as he chooses, but I am very different, and will not take orders as to thee, from him or anybody else. Thou art my mistress and not his. And she shook her head, and she said, very gently: Nay, thou dost not understand. I am not anybody's mistress. I am my own mistress, and do exactly as I please, whether he or any other like it or not. There lives not the man who shall say to me: Here is a line, and over it, thou shalt not step. And whatever I do, I do, of my own free will, not of obedience, but of my own consent. I have given my body and soul away, but my will is mine.

And I said with emphasis: I have bought thee at the price of a kingdom, and become a beggar on thy account, and mine thou art, by right. Dost thou actually tell me, I am to lose my kingdom, and get absolutely nothing in exchange? And she said, always with the same sweet and quiet voice, whose tone never varied, adding by the very charm of its gentle music fire to the exasperating sting that lay in the words it said: I have nothing at all to do with thy kingdom, and if thou hast lost it, I am very sorry: yet blame not me for its loss, but thyself alone, for the choice was thine. And moreover, I am not for sale. I give myself, or part of me, to anyone I choose. It is for dealers and merchants to bargain. I never bargain. I am a Queen. And I said in wrath: Thou shalt give thyself no longer to anyone but me. Thou hast already cheated me by making me the loser in a bargain where I lose all, gaining nothing in exchange. But I will have either my kingdom or thyself: and if not the kingdom, which is gone, then thee. And she said quietly: Say nothing rash, or harsh, or ill-considered. It is not I that have cheated thee out of thy kingdom: it is no one but thyself.

And I exclaimed: What! didst thou not cheat me by telling me thou didst love me long ago? And she broke in instantly, and said: I said nothing of the kind: it is thy own imagination. I never told thee anything so false as that I loved thee. And I said: Nay, not in words, but in a language deeper far than any words. What woman ever gave a man what thou hast given me, without telling him very plainly, he was the object of her love? And she said quietly: It was but thy own inference, and utterly unwarranted. And I said: Why didst thou then allow me to make love to thee at all? And she said, very gently: I did not ask, nor even wish thee, to make love to me at all. But I was touched by thy emotion, and thy passion, and thy miserable longing, and willing to soothe it, and gratify it, for an instant, letting thee taste that nectar for which thou wert so obviously dying: for I am kind.

And I exclaimed with a shout: Kind! Why, what is thy kindness but the very extremity of unkindness? What! and did all thy caresses mean absolutely nothing? And she said, very gently: They meant exactly what they were, gifts and boons, bestowed of sheer compassion: and if from their receipt, thou hast drawn the conclusion that thy affection was returned, it is not so: it is only thy own unjustified construction, for thou art not, and never can be, anything to me, but the thing that thou wilt not be, a mere friend. And I said: What kind of a woman art thou to betray me with kisses? And she said: I am only what I am: but thou art most unfair to me, and instead of peevishly demanding of me what I cannot give, and growing so unreasonably angry, thou oughtest rather to be very grateful to me, for giving thee anything at all. I told thee almost as soon as I had seen thee, in the very beginning of all, that I belonged, body and soul, to Narasinha: and yet notwithstanding, I took pity on thee, for thy misery, and gave thee, by concession, what I might very easily have refused, humouring thy weakness like that of a child, crying for what he cannot have. But never did I promise thee anything beyond: and I even told thee, if thou canst remember it, that it might injure thee and could not do thee any good. But thou wert blind, and as it were buried in thy dream. Did I not warn thee, and entreat thee beforehand, not to blame me, when the dream was over, and reality returned? And when I had surfeited thy longing, and dismissed thee, I meant it to be the end, for it was all I had to give. In all, it is not I, that have in any way whatever deceived thee: thou hast all along only deceived thyself. And if I have deceived at all, it is myself alone I have deceived, by expecting any gratitude for the boon of my compassion, and the favour that I poured on thee with no miser's band, because I blamed myself for being innocently guilty of becoming the unintentional object of thy passion, and its involuntary cause.

XXVIII

And I listened, so utterly confounded by the very simplicity of her apology, which overturned all my accusations, and put me in the wrong, that I stood in silence, unable to find anything to say. And in my stupefaction, I began to laugh. And I said: Ha! Nectar when she turns towards thee: poison when she turns away! Hast thou never heard the Queen's verse? And she said: What! wilt thou actually lay on me the burden of refuting the silly slander of a rhyme, circulated by little rascals merely for want of something else to say? Can I help what they say, or shall I even stoop to listen when they say it, who will say anything of queens, without shame for the envious venom of their own base insignificance, knowing all the time absolutely nothing, but making mere noise, like frogs all croaking together in a marsh? Or if I must absolutely answer, in spite of my disdain, how can I prevent any lover, such as thyself, from persuading himself of what he wishes to believe? For all of them resemble thee, behaving like unreasonable bulls, the very moment that they see me, and pestering me like flies, to my torment, and yet would blame me for driving them away. And every one of them, exactly like thee, imagines me his own, for no reason that I am ever able to discover, although I tell them all, exactly as I told thee, that I belong to Narasinha.

And I said in wrath: I will slice off the head of Narasinha, by and by, as I have done already for some of his tools. And I will not be the plaything of a moment, to be cast aside the next. I have lost a kingdom for thy sake, and will have thee to repay me, whether thou wilt or no. And she said with a smile: Thou art angry, and talking nonsense in thy anger, as angry men will. Dost thou not see that thou art bereft of thy senses? For, kingdom or no kingdom, how canst thou be so silly as to propose to force me, willy nilly, to love thee when I do not love? If I loved thee, I should say so, and all force would be superfluous: if not, it would be not only useless, but injurious to thy own cause, seeing that the more thou forcest, the less wilt thou obtain: nay, whereas now thou art indifferent, thou wilt bring it about that I shall hate thee in the end, as I am beginning to do a very little even now. And then it will be worse for thee in every way. For thou dost not seem ever to remember that I am, after all, not only a woman, but a queen.

And I looked at her as she spoke, saying to myself: She is wrong, for nobody looking at her ever could forget it, even for a moment, just because, like the grace of a lily, it is forgotten by herself, and she would still be a queen, even if she were not a queen at all. And she looks at me, notwithstanding the biting reproof in her words, with exactly the same intoxicating and caressing sweetness, as if I were still a dear friend with whom she were unwilling to quarrel. And I gazed at her, yearning towards her with every fibre of my soul, and yet exasperated almost beyond endurance at the thought that she was keeping me like a stranger at a distance from her heart, in order to preserve it for another. And after a while, I said slowly: If thy affection is not to be given to me, it shall never be given to anybody else. And she said, as if with curiosity: Thou art surely mad. For how canst thou prevent any other from following thy own example, and doing just what thou hast done thyself, losing thy reason at the sight of me, as all men always do? Dost thou not see that my power to excite affection is far greater than thine to prevent it? And I said: It would be very very easy for me to prevent all others from ever loving thee again.

And she looked at me with eyes, in whose unruffled calm there was not even the faintest shadow of any fear. And she said quietly: I understand thee very well, and yet for all that I tell thee thou art raving, and thou art, without knowing it, very like the very man thou hatest most, Narasinha. For often he has said to me the very same thing that thou art saying now: and yet, though according to thee, the thing is very easy, he finds it so difficult as to be utterly impossible. For he cannot endure to do without me, even in a dream, and cannot therefore bring himself to slay me, as he is constantly threatening to do, knowing very well that he might rather slay himself, since once I am gone, he will never find another me, to put in my place. And this is true, even though I cannot understand it: just as I cannot understand what it is that makes me indispensable to thee or to anybody else. For I know it only by its effect. And so I am my own protection, against all his threats, or thine. And if I had thought otherwise, what could have been easier, since thou talkest of easy things, than to have summoned my attendants and bade them put thee out, when it may be, thy life would have paid for thy marvellous impertinence, in intruding unbidden, as perhaps it still may, without any instigation of my own at all? Thou dost not seem to understand that all this while thy own life is in far greater danger than mine; since thou hast done a thing that will not be forgiven thee by others, though I myself have not only forgiven thee, but well understanding the fiery goad that drove thee into my presence, have treated thee, for yet once more, with kindness and condescension far beyond any deserts of thine. And for all return, thou art threatening even to slay me. But I am destitute of fear.

And she stood before me in the moonlight, that turned her as it clung to all her limbs into a thing beautiful beyond all earthly dreams, absolutely fearless, and with a dignity whose royalty was not only that of a queen, but of loveliness laughing to scorn all possible comparison, seeming to say without the need of any words: Art thou brave enough, and fool enough, to lay rude hands on such a thing as I am, or even if thy folly were equal to thy courage, canst thou find it in thy heart to think of violence offered to it, by thyself or any other, even in a dream? And my heart burned, for sheer adoration, and yet strange! it began to sink at the very same time, as I gazed at her, looking at me quietly in return. For there was something absolutely unanswerable, not only in herself, but in everything she said, and yet her very simplicity that overwhelmed me with its soft irrefutable sweetness increased the torture of my hopeless admiration every time she spoke. And suddenly I struck my hands together in despair. And I exclaimed: Ah! thou marvel of a woman and a queen, I am conquered by thee, and I am on the very verge of falling at thy feet in a passion of tears, craving thy forgiveness as a criminal, so bewildering is the double spell of thy beauty and thy intelligence, and the candour of thy strange soul, which drives me mad with its inexplicable charm. But what does it matter to me, hate me or love me, if I am never to see thee any more? Aye! Narasinha may not find it in him to slay thee for thy wayward and beautiful independence, but then he can see thee every day, exactly as he chooses: whereas I, once I go away this night, am outcast: for well I understand that thou or he will see to it that I never come again. Dost thou imagine I can bear it? And again I struck my hands together with a cry. And I exclaimed: Curse on my birth, and the crimes of the births that went before it, that I was not born Narasinha! for he has cut me from my happiness, and stolen from me the very fruit of being born at all!

And in my frenzy, I seized her in my arms once more, desperately clutching, as it were, at the bliss escaping from my reach in her form. And I said to her, as I held her tight: Tell me, had Narasinha never lived, could I have been to thee what he is now? And she extricated herself, very gently, from my arms, and stood back, looking at me with meditative eyes; and after a while, she said doubtfully, yet with a little smile on her lips: Perhaps. But I am not sure. Thou art a little over-bearing. And yet I like thee, somehow, but I love thee not at all. And yet again, it may be, that had I met thee sooner, I might have looked at thee with other eyes. And I bear thee no malice, if indeed thou art a criminal, for any of thy crimes, since I was their occasion. But what after all is the use of supposition as to what might be were Narasinha away, since as it is, he is here, an obstacle in the way, not to be surmounted by any means whatever? And so, thy case is hopeless. And I tried to make thee understand, in vain: since thou wilt not take denial or listen to any reason. And I went to such a length, out of kindness, as to give thee one single evening, packed as full as it could hold with all the sweetness I could think of, giving myself up, so to say, to the insatiable thirst of thy arms, and thy craving desire to be caressed and kissed by only me, and embodying thy dream, and turning myself into an instrument of that nectar of feminine intoxication for which thou wert ready to die, and putting myself without reserve absolutely at thy disposal, only to find my kindness miserably requited by ingratitude and undeserved reproaches, and even menaces and threats. And as I said, to-night, when by underhand contrivance thou didst force thyself upon me, I never punished thee at all, as many another queen might do, but took pity on thy desolation and forgave and overlooked all thy insolence, without being in the very least deceived by thy fustian beginning, which I easily discerned to be a *ruse*, to enable thee perhaps to steal back into my favour, all founded on a misinterpretation of the woman that I am. For had I really been what people say, and what, listening to them, thou didst imagine me, thy foolish plan might perhaps have been successful, but I am very different indeed. And yet, even so, thy part was played so poorly, that it failed almost as soon as it began, since it needed but a touch of my finger to make thee drop thy mask, and reveal thyself to be, what all the time I knew thee, a lover in the depths of despair. For love is very hard to hide, and thou couldst scarcely hope to deceive even those who are very easy to deceive, as I am not. And as I watched thy clumsy effort, sitting as it did so ill on one so simple and direct as thou art, I could not prevent my compassion from mixing with a very little laughter, remembering the ass in the Panchatantra, who clothed him in a lion's skin, forgetting that his ears betrayed him, to say nothing of his voice. And now for the second time I have given thee something that I would have refused thee altogether, had caresses of compassion been any argument of love. But understand well, that there will be no third opportunity: for this is thy farewell. Go as thou hast come, for I will not attempt to penetrate thy secret, nor have thy footsteps dogged.

XXIX

And as I listened, I knew that all was over, and that her words were my doom: for I understood that she was stronger far than I, and in a position absolutely impregnable by any efforts I might make. And I stood gazing at her silently with a tumult in my soul that could find no utterance in words. And I said at last, in a very low voice: Is thy decision irrevocable, and am I really never to see thee any more? And she said: Even this time is more than I had allowed thee, and I am afraid for thee. Aye! I fear that thy life is the forfeit thou wilt pay. Yet blame not me for anything that may occur. For Narasinha would have slain thee already, as he is furiously jealous of anything that comes near me in the form of a man, had I not myself expressly interfered in thy behalf, making him swear to overlook thy former trespass on a ground that he considers as his own. But he will not listen to me now. And to-morrow, as soon as he discovers what has taken place to-night, for I cannot hide it, he will take measures to prevent thy ever coming back, very likely such as thou thyself hinted at, of me, a little while ago. Thou art looking at me now for the very last time; and remember, I told thee myself, I will take no blame, if thy temerity turns out to have cost thee dear. Farewell, and if thou canst, forget me, and go away to a great distance, without the loss of a single moment. For in a very little while, thou mayst find, there will not even be the chance, and it will be too late.

And instead of going, I stood, rooted to the spot like a tree, gazing at her thirstily, in a stupor of despair, and saying to myself: What! can it really be possible that I am actually looking at her now, as she says, for the very last time in my life, doomed to go here, or there, in the world, without ever seeing her again, knowing all the while that she is, still, somewhere to be seen, and actually being seen, only not by me? Out upon such horror, for it would be less, even if she were dead! And she, so kind, so gentle, how in the world can she stand there, bidding me with a wave of her hand, in that low sweet voice of hers, to go away to a great distance, to save my life, knowing well, for she is very clever, that she is taking it away, by banishing me for ever? And am I just to be thrown away at the bidding of Narasinha?

And at the thought, all at once I began to laugh with sheer rage. And I said to myself: What! must I turn my back on heaven, and go meekly down to hell, at the order of Narasinha? Would she banish me at all, but for Narasinha? Who in the world is Narasinha? Is Narasinha my master? Is he even her master, for as it seems, she is rather his? Are these his orders, or her own? Ha! now, I wonder. What if after all this Narasinha were only a man of straw, doing exactly as he is told, and acting as her agent and her instrument, for the sake of what she gives him? Is it likely, after all, that he orders, and she obeys? And am I being fooled, and handed over by herself to banishment, or even death, behind the screen of Narasinha?

And I looked at her as she stood, patiently waiting for me to go, with a soul torn to pieces by rage, and suspicion, and love-longing, and flat refusal to go away. And suddenly there came into my recollection Haridása, saying as he stood outside the door: Nectar when she turns towards thee: poison when she turns away. And I said to myself: So now, she turns away. And can she possibly not know, what becomes of all her lovers?

And I went up to her, all at once, and took her by her two hands, and looked straight into her eyes. And I said: Táráwalí, thou choosest thy servants well. I know the use of Chaturiká. And now dimly I begin to see the use of Narasinha. Does he never tell thee where he throws the bodies of thy old lovers, when thou hast finished with their souls?

And then, strange! her eyes wavered, as if unable to meet my own. And like a flash of lightning, I understood. And I exclaimed: Ha! have I found at last the question that thou canst not answer, and laid my finger on the flaw in thy consummate skill? So then, this was all but a comedy that thou wert playing, to shift the blame from thy own shoulders and turn me over to extinction at the hands of Narasinha? Ah! thou art thy own mistress, and not one to obey. But ah! thou lovely lady that hast no pity for thy poisoned lovers, it is not the lover this time that shall die. And thou shalt meet thy master for the first time in thy life.

And I looked at her for a single instant in a frenzy of fierce hatred that suddenly blazed up from the ashes of my dead devotion, lying scorned and cheated and betrayed by the idol it adored. And I seized her in the grip of death, and tore from my arm the lute-string that was wound about my wrist. And I said: Dear, I never gave thee thy music-lesson: but now I will give thee a very long one on a single string. And in an instant, I twisted it about her neck, and drew it tight, holding her still as she struggled, in an ecstasy of giant strength. And so I stood, trembling all over, for a very long time. And at last, I felt that she lay in my arms like a dead weight, hanging as it were against her will in the terrible embrace of a lover that loved with hatred instead of love.

And I laid her down very gently, turning carefully away, that I might not see her face. And I went away very quickly, and all at once, as I went, I fell down and began to sob, as if my heart would break. And at last, after a long while, I got up, and stood, thinking, and looking back under the trees. And I crept back on tiptoe, and looked and saw her at a distance, lying in the moonlight, very still, like the tomb of my own heart. And then I turned sharp round, and went away for good and all, without a soul. And I said to myself in agony: Now I have made the whole world empty with my own hand, and it was myself that I have killed, as well as her. And now I will go after her as soon as I possibly can. But there is one thing still to do, before I go, for I have to give another lesson to Narasinha. Only this time I will not use a lute-string, but crush out his soul with my bare hands.

Ha! Narasinha, I have told thee, and thou knowest all. And now thou hast only to count the hours that are left to thee, for I am coming very soon.

FOOTNOTES:

[6] Pronounce in three syllables *Shut-roon-jye*: it means, *one who triumphs over his foes*. So again, in three syllables, *Narasing*: which means, *man-lion*, alluding to one of Wishnu's incarnations. (Europeans do not adequately realise that the short final *a*, in Sanskrit, is always mute. They pronounce e.g. *Ráma*, *Krishna*, as if the last letter were long. They are monosyllables.)

[7] "The menace prevented the deed," observes Gibbon, of a would-be assassin of Commodus. That was also the error of the Germans, in 1914.

[8] A heavenly musician.

[9] *Dharma* does not mean religion in our sense of the word. It means, for every man, that set of obligations laid on him by his caste or status: thus everybody's *dharma* is different.

[10] A crown prince. Palace intrigues were common in the old Hindoo courts. Each wife thought of nothing but providing the heir to the throne, if not by fair means, then by foul.

[11] Krishna, the lute-player, and flute-player, *par excellence*. He resembles Odin in this particular.

[12] i.e. *the city of lotuses*. The final *a* is mute.

[13] i.e. *a line of stars*; *a constellation*; *a star intensified*.

[14] That is to say, abandoned, dissolute: independence being, in old Hindoo ears, a synonym for every possible species of depravity.

[15] There is here an untranslatable play on *mánasa* and *manasi-já* = a feminine god of love.

[16] There is no vulgarity in this idea: it is a poetical degree in the scale of passion. An *abhisáriká* is a lady so mastered by her love that she cannot wait for her lover, but goes to him of her own accord. There are all sorts of

conditions laid down to regulate her going: she must not go in broad daylight, but in a thunderstorm, or dusk.

[17] *Láwanya* means loveliness as well as salt.

[18] The exact equivalent, and indeed the only possible translation of *kupanditá.*

[19] This is due to the peculiar dress of Hindoo women, all in one piece, and put on so that the edge that runs around the feet afterwards runs up diagonally and winds around the whole figure. No national costume was ever better calculated to set off the sinuosities and soft grace of a woman's figure to advantage than the marvellous simplicity of the *sarí* which is nothing more than a very long strip of almost anything you please.

[20] i.e. *the clever one*: a name, like Nipuniká, employed in Hindoo plays to denote the qualities of a *grisette*: *Suzanne.*

[21] *Anuraktámritam bálá wiraktá wisham ewa sá.*

[22] A female door-keeper. This appears to have been customary in old times. Runjeet Singh had a body-guard of women, dressed like boys.

[23] The roots of these great figs "grow down" (hence their name) from the branches, often coalescing with the trunks into the most extraordinary shapes: it needs no imagination to see Dryads under the bark: they are visible to the naked eye. The huge leaves and great white blossom of the *shála* make it one of the most beautiful of earthly trees: as the champak is one of the most weird, like a great candlestick of innumerable branches whose pale flower-cups grow out of the end of its clumsy fingers without leaves.

[24] Durgá, *the inaccessible one*, is one of Párwatí's innumerable names. It has reference to a mountain steep, with accessory meanings, moral and theological.

[25] There are constant references in Hindoo poetry to swinging, which is a national pastime in India, with a special festival in its honour.

[26] Pronounce as a trisyllable: Haridás.

[27] The Indian women used to send little earthenware dishes, with a lighted wick in their oil, floating down the Ganges, to symbolise their children's lives. Perhaps they do it still: but all these beautiful old superstitious practices are dying away, in the light of "representative institutions." New lamps for old ones!

[28] That is Shrí, the Hindoo Aphrodite. Only those who have studied Hindoo goddesses on the old temple walls, where they stand with

everlasting marble smiles in long silent rows, buried in the jungles that encircle their deserted fanes, will enter into the atmosphere of this strange description.

[29] *Daiwatam hi hayottamah*, says Somadewa: *a good horse is a divine thing.*

[30] The Hindoo Æsculapius. Ayurweda, the science of medicine.

[31] A gem that attracts straws, presumably amber. It is always employed by Hindoo poets as an equivalent of our *magnet.*

[32] *i.e.* the mirage.

[33] That is, as if she were a character in a play, coming at her cue. The phrase is common in the Hindoo plays.

[34] This is due to the coal-black stem, which gives to a palm tree shorn of its head the look of a tumble-down smoke-grimed chimney. Unshorn, leaning to the wind, it is the most graceful thing in the world, especially seen against the setting sun.

[35] The great jewel on Wishnu's breast.

[36] Literally, with a *sáshtanganamaskara*: i.e. *with an obeisance made by falling prostrate with the eight corners of the body*, a form of profound reverence made as to a divinity.

III
A STORY WITHOUT AN END

And then, Maheshwara tossed the last leaf into the air. And as it floated away down the stream, he said to the goddess, as she listened with attention: And yet he never came, as I told thee at the beginning. For Narasinha was beforehand with him, after all.

And the Daughter of the Snow sat silent, looking away down the river after the floating leaf, until it was lost to sight. And then she said slowly: Why didst thou say in the beginning that Táráwalí was the most extraordinary of all women, past, present, or to come? For I was deceived by thy encomium, expecting a woman altogether different from her, who was only but a specimen of her sex.

And the Moony-crested god burst into loud laughter. And he exclaimed: Speak low, O Snowy One: for if thy mortal sisters overheard thee betraying their secrets and their cause, they would be very angry, and perhaps begin to curse thee as a traitor, instead of offering thee worship, as they all do now. What! dost thou actually deem her to be but a type of all the rest? Surely, thou must have been asleep all the time that I was reading, after all: since thou hast either misunderstood her altogether, or it may be, wilt not do her justice, out of jealousy: since no woman in the three worlds can ever be trusted to judge another fairly, treating her always as a criminal and a rival, and falling on her tooth and nail, especially if, like Táráwalí, she sets custom at defiance, going by an independent standard of her own. But now, let me help thee to see how utterly mistaken is thy estimate of a character so rare as hardly to be matched in the whole of space and time for her cleverness and her candour and her tranquillity of soul, leaving her beauty out of the account, as that one element in her common to a very host of others. For the Creator was not such a bungler as to confine all feminine beauty to a single instance, but scattered it universally, since almost every woman in the world, no matter what her face be like, shares in the wonderful fascination exerted over men by the shape essential to her sex, which is far the most important thing of all, being general instead of special, as every woman seen dimly in the dark, or at a distance, or with her face hidden by a veil, will prove, being then above all most attractive when her face cannot be seen at all: as the story that I told thee of the ugly lady, not long ago, shows, if thou hast not forgotten it.[37] Whereas the thing special to Táráwalí was her incomparable soul, in which were mingled elements hardly ever to be found combined, gentleness and strength, and simplicity almost naive, with subtlety beyond all comparison, and pride that never took offence, and superlative beauty with humility, and submissiveness with extreme independence of spirit, and kindness without weakness, and feminine sweetness of disposition with the intellectual vigour of a man, and his courage, and his candour, all of which combined with her extraordinary bodily beauty to make her a paragon of intoxication utterly irresistible to every male[38] she came across, like a very Prakriti in a woman's form.

And Párwatí said: How canst thou lavish such praise on a woman so deservedly slain by her infuriated lover, when he suddenly awoke to the discovery of the real nature behind the mask?

And the great god laughed again, and he looked at her shrewdly and he said: Aha! Snowy One, said I not that thou wert asleep as I read? I shall have to repeat to thee the story all over again another time. Dost thou actually not see that all she said, from beginning to end, was absolutely true? For Shatrunjaya told the whole story very well, as he understood it; but he did not understand completely, and made a terrible error in the most important point of all, being led astray by what he had heard, and easily taken in. For blinded by his rage against his rival Narasinha, he came suddenly to the wrong conclusion, and slew her by mistake, never so much as giving her time for any explanation. For her eyes never wavered, as he thought, for guilt, but for quite another reason. And Narasinha really was, exactly as she said, her tyrant, nor had she anything to do with his assassination of her lovers, which he committed all on his own account, out of jealousy, paying no attention at all to her intercession. But in her gentleness, she shrank from the very idea of any violence, and this was the true cause of the wavering of her eyes, foreseeing as she did another attempt on Shatrunjaya, which she could not avert. And my heart was grieved at her death at the hands of a lover whose life she had saved, and would have saved again if she could. For she was worth far more than he.

And the Daughter of the Snow said: But what was she doing with such a multitude of lovers at all?

And Maheshwara said: Thou art like Shatrunjaya himself, biased against her by the insinuations of Haridása, and the discreditable behaviour of that little liar Chaturiká, who betrayed her as well as others, and by the idle talk of the people, which she rightly compared herself to the croaking of so many frogs. For low people always put the very worst interpretation upon the actions of kings, and especially of queens, of whom all the time they know less than nothing, exactly as she said. And Shatrunjaya's opinion of her wavered, in spite of all his worship, being coloured by the scandal that he heard, so that he saw her through its mist, as strangers always do. And if she had too many lovers, it was all the fault of the Creator, who endowed her with such fascination, combined with the kindness of her heart: since she blamed herself for their misery, and could not bear to send them away without making them as it were some reparation for her crime of being beautiful beyond all resistance. And this was her only fault.

Then said the Mountain-born, with emphasis: I hate her: for a woman should confine herself to one.

And Maheshwara said, looking at her with affection: Ah! Snowy One, thou art right, and thou art wrong. For not every woman is a counterpart of thee. And moreover, to be rigidly inaccessible[39] is terribly hard, when a woman is as she was, a very incarnation of bewildering intoxication, and kind into the bargain. For then she resembles a fortress, besieged night and day and mined everlastingly by innumerable hosts absolutely determined to get in; and sleepless indeed must be the garrison that guards it; and often it yields of sheer weariness and fatigue, unable any longer to endure the strain. And Táráwalí was absolutely right when she said that her lovers drove her, against her inclination, into the reputation of a lady of many lovers, since they were all so infatuated by the very sight of her that they never let her alone. For love that really finds its object will face ten thousand deaths to reach it, and is very hard to repel. And it laughs in utter scorn at arguments, and bribes, and barriers, and dangers, and refusals, bent with a burning heart upon one thing only, to reach its goal, dead or alive, no matter which. And when a woman is an incarnation of that object, she moves the whole world with her little finger, and is fatal, and raised into a category above all ordinary rules. And Táráwalí was moreover in a peculiar position, for her husband had thrown her away of his own accord, so that she actually belonged to nobody but herself, and injured herself alone, if she could not always help yielding when a lover pushed her terribly hard, by touching her heart like Shatrunjaya in the matter of his dream. And very few indeed are the women who would not have done the same, for he was a great musician, and a man among men, and very young. And very rare indeed is the woman who is qualified to censure her. For most women keep their wheel upon the track, either because nobody ever tries to make them leave it, or simply for fear, either of being punished, or of other women's tongues. And not one in a crore could have resisted half the pressure that Táráwalí had to bear, for the very greatest of a winning woman's charms is exactly the one which she possessed in supreme perfection, her soft and delicious willingness to oblige and please, and place all the sweetness of her personality at the absolute disposal of her lover, as Shatrunjaya understood at the very first sight of her: a thing so utterly irresistible, that when it is combined, as it was in her, with intelligence masculine in its quality, its owner sweeps away every man's reason like a chip in a flood. And there was a special reason for Táráwalí's intelligence.

And the goddess said: What was the reason? And the Moony-crested god said: It was the necessary consequence of the actions of a former birth. For in the birth before, she was a man, doomed by *gati*[40] to become a woman in the next, by reason of a sin. And she said again: What sin? Then said Maheshwara: Ask me another time, O thou cajoler: for it is a long story, and now I have no more leisure: since I must go and bestow the favour of my presence on a ceremony performed by a pious devotee who has built me a new temple at Wáránasi. And canst thou guess who it is?

And the Daughter of the Snow said: How in the world can I guess his name, of whom I never heard before?

And the Moony-crested god said: It is not a he, but a she: being no other than Tárávalí herself, in yet another birth. And she is still only a woman, for she has not yet succeeded in raising herself by merit into the condition of a man. And it may be long before she succeeds. For it is easy to sink, but it is hard for any creature to rise into a status of being superior to its own, and the women who emerge into manhood are very rare. For the goodness that is synonymous with real existence[41] is only to be found in those who have behind them the accumulated effort and desert of ages, standing on a peak loftier by far than any of thy father's snowy summits, which cannot be attained in any single birth by no matter what exertions or austerities. But when once any being has attained it, emancipation dawns, touching it into colour more beautiful by far than any tints the rising sun has ever thrown on newly fallen mountain snow.

FOOTNOTES:

[37] A very beautiful story in the MS., which has not yet seen the light. The opinion of the deity is corroborated by that very clever woman, Lady Mary Wortley Montagu, who says in one of her letters from Constantinople that if women went without clothes, the face would hardly count at all. Nearly all of them would gain immensely by wearing a permanent veil, but the pretty ones would never consent to it.

[38] Purusha is the philosophical term for the Primordial Male, of which Prakriti is the female antithesis. The god is combining Goethe and Swinburne: the "eternal feminine" and the "holy spirit of man."

[39] See note *ante*, p. 47.

[40] A very short word for a very long process, and untranslatable by any English equivalent. It means the whole system of the laws of metempsychosis, running in a long chain forward into the future, and back into the past.

[41] That is, *sat* or *sattwa* = goodness, or true being.